THE FIRST MAN OFF THE PLANE

By

David O. Strickland

EDWARD R. MURROW: You didn't expect to return as a hero?

GENERAL WILLIAM F. DEAN: No, anything but that, I expected when I returned that I might have even been court-martialed for not having done better; for not fulfilling my obligations to my country.

--- From a CBS Broadcast, October 3, 1953

"Hello."

"Hello, may I speak with Mrs. King, Mrs. King?" It was Ike Tapem on the telephone speaking from the White House, the one in Washington, D. C.

"This is she."

"The President would like to see you for some photo opportunities. "

"I don't need any." Mrs. King hung up.

It was ten o'clock in the morning in the Florida panhandle. Mrs. King had already rolled her hair in curlers, each curler the size of a Budweiser can. The time had come for the start of the serious business of the day--the serious business being the mixing and drinking of a gin and tonic. Mrs. King called this drink a gin and quinine water. The ice came from a large electric icebox that magically produces and presents ice cubes. No need to open the door. Just push a button and bang there comes an ice cube. Push the button twice and bang-bang there come two ice cubes. Magic. Sometimes the magic doesn't work and the icebox wets the floor. A lot of mildew grows in the corners of Mrs. King's kitchen.

"Hello."

"Hello, Mrs. King? I am Ike Tapem, the appointments secretary to the President of the United States of America, Mr. Nixon." He was an assistant appointments secretary.

"Dear God. "

"We got cut off a minute ago." Ike Tapem knew full well that they weren't cut off.

"We did?"

"I think that you misunderstood me. The President wants to see you at the White House and have his picture taken with you."

"I thought that you were trying to sell me one of them 98-

Cent color portraits."

"The President wants to see you and have his picture taken with you." Tapem said the word his as though it had a capital H.

"Mercy, why? Say, you're not putting me on are you?"

"I am dead serious. You can come to Washington, can't you?"

"Oh my. I--well, I guess I can--let me see, yes--I can. Say, who would pay for such a thing? The POW wives' club?"

"An Air Force car will pick you up in one hour and take you to-- I think it is Eglin."

"That's what they call it, Eglin Air Force Base."

"Umm, a White House jet will be waiting. You will be in Washington within two hours. You'll be home in time for supper."

"Heavens, I don't know if I can make it that soon or not.

What'll I wear? Will a pants suit look OK? "

Ike Tapem didn't know it, but a pants suit couldn't possibly look good on anyone as large and lumpy as Mrs. King; an oversight that would get him in trouble with the President of the United States of America. Mr. Tapem spoke from ignorance when he said,

"Sure, OK, and if you need your hair done, you can have it done here.

"Oh, I always wear one of my wigs."

"Quite. "

"Look Mister. I think I'd better come tomorrow. This is all too sudden, besides the ladies have the spa this afternoon. I want to look good when Rex comes home." Mrs. King weighs 212 pounds naked. She stands 5 feet 2 inches tall.

"The President--. Ma'am, when the President wants to see someone he sees them. Besides he might go to San Clemente or maybe Key Biscayne this evening to spend the holidays. The car will be there in 56 minutes. Good-bye, Mrs. King." It was Mr. Tapem's turn to hang up.

As she heard the click, an important question popped into Mrs. King's mind. She picked up her pink princess touch-tone telephone and dialed the operator. She didn't dial really; she pushed the operator button. One doesn't dial a touch-tone telephone; one pushes. Just how many princesses own princess touch-tone telephones is something that I really couldn't say.

I can say that Mrs. King had to push quite hard as the buttons stick. They stick from their daily dose of gin and quinine water. Mrs. King often pushes with one hand whilst she spills with the other. The sugar in the quinine water makes the buttons stick.

The telephone smells like a gin-drinking princess.

"Operator 94."

"I want to place a call to Mr. Eisenhower Tatem at the White House, that's the one in Washington, D.C., Operator 94."

"Do you want a person to person call?"

"Yeah"

"You can dial that direct. First dial 'O', then the area code, then the number."

"I don't know the number."

"First dial the area code, then 555-1212."

"I don't know the fucking area code." Mrs. King was someone to reckon with.

"You will find a listing of area codes in the front of your directory." A directory is what telephone operators call a phone book.

"Listen, operator 94, I'm going to see the fucking President of the United States of America in three hours. Besides, my husband is a fucking POW." Mrs. King was not quite right about either man's sexual habits, but never mind.

"Sorry Madame, why didn't you say so in the first place? How was I to know? Who'd you all say you wanted to talk with?"

"Eisenhower Batem, the White House."

"Just a moment, please." Time goes by.

"What the fuck is taking so long?"

"They say that there is no Eisenhower Cakem at the White

House, Miss. They want to know if that is a cover name. "
"Mother of God, try Ike Blakem, he is some sort of a secretary to the President. He is a man, but he said he was a secretary."

"Oh, you mean Ike Tapem." A third voice was on the line.

"Yes, that's it." Mrs. King got the name right this time.

"Yes, this is Ike Tapem."

"Just a minute. Are you paid, operator?"

It was that third voice watching the public's money.

"For shit sakes, do you think I'd call the fucking goddamn White House collect?"

"Go ahead please."

"Mr.Tatum?

"This is Ike Tapem. "

"Well, this is Regina King."

"Yes, yes Mrs. King."

"What I want to know is can I get my nails done when I get there?"

"Your what?"

"My nails."

"Oh yes, of course you can. The White House maintains a beauty parlor in the basement for the family and Rose Mary Wood and people like yourself."

"Sounds classy."

"It is."

"Make me an appointment in a couple of hours, Mr. Appointments

Secretary. Good-bye. "

It was Mrs. King's turn to hang up.

"Ringling Brothers Barnum and Bailey," said Ike Tapem out loud to himself. The assistant appointments secretary had never dealt with the President before and today was his big day. It was a Saturday, and it was the most important day in Tapem's life.

He wore his best suit, his best tie and his best shirt. He looked like a middle-aged bar mitzvah boy. His shoes squeaked when he walked.

The President had a free day this day--no appointments. Tapem was to sit around all day outside the oval office in case Mr. Nixon wanted to make an appointment with Anwar el-Sadat or Leonid Brezhnev or Chairman Mao or Teddy Heath or Francisco Franco or Howard Hughes or Pope Paul or Billy Graham or someone from The National Enquirer.

So far the only word from the President had been relayed via H.R. "Bob" Haldeman. "The President wants to have his picture taken with one of those POW wives. You know, one of the attractive ones, wholesome mid-west types. Someone, something that will show his support for the POWs and what a fine American he is. A few nice looking kids would be nice. Have them here at two."

"Right."

Tapem picked up his telephone and shouted at the White House switchboard, "Get me the POW Affairs Officer at the Pentagon-- Admiral whosit, you know." The Pentagon is a five sided building frequented by admirals and generals. It is across the Potomac River from Washington.

Time goes by.

"The Admiral is in California at the meeting of the POW Wives and Families Association or something like that."

"Let me talk to him there. "

"They don't know where he is staying. They suggest you try the Executive Secretary of the POW Wives and Families Association,

Dick Westcott."

The Admiral was with Dick Westcott. In fact Dick Westcott was treating the Admiral and himself to two $200-a--night call girls and were at that moment trying to get their money's worth.

Fat chance.

Tapem told the Admiral what he wanted.

The Admiral said, "Sure."

"Good, give me a name and I'll take it from there."

"I'll call you next Tuesday when I get back to the Pentagon. I'm very busy right now." The Admiral wasn't as busy as the call girl. The call girl was trying to make the Admiral have an erection.

"But we need one this afternoon at two."

"LA time or Washington time?" That sort of question gets one ahead in a Naval career.

"Washington."

"Just can't be done. They're all in LA, right down to the last tit."

"Jesus. The color left Tapem's face. His chance to shine turned dim. He reached for a sip of coffee. His mouth was dry. His hand trembled. "You must have someone. You must. The President--The President—I mean..."

"Hey Westcott, what's the name of that canary all the other broads are raising hell about? You know the one the computer forgot to notify? Right. Regina King. She's the only dame not in LA."

And so it was. Mrs. King was the only POW wife that could possibly get to the White House on time. Tapem took it upon himself and ordered a White House jet. He found Mrs. King and she agreed to come. Tapem smiled. He looked ever so satisfied. He had pulled it off. It worked. It really did. This was truly his big day. Now the President wanted to see him in person right in the oval office. A greater honor could not be had. He stood up and straightened his tie. He held his hand up to his mouth and blew, testing his breath. He smelt of menthol cigarettes-- stale menthol cigarettes. No matter, he wouldn't blow in Mr. Nixon's face. He glanced down at his shirt. It was spotted with spilt coffee.

At the north end of Friendship of Nations Road stands the Hanoi Hilton. Don't let the name Hanoi Hilton fool you. It is not a hotel. It is a prison, the Hoa Lo Prison. If the road called Friendship of Nations is unfamiliar, don't be alarmed. It is the old Avenue Louis Napoleon. The North Vietnamese changed the names of most of the streets in Hanoi once the French left in

1954. The name of the Hoa Lo Prison was never officially changed, but the guests, the prisoners that is, and the then President Nixon called it the Hanoi Hilton. They were not so authorized by Mr. Hilton. Mr. Hilton is the man that lets hotels use his name if the hotel will guarantee that all its bathrooms will be clean and that all its bars will serve dry martinis. It is hard to understand, I know, but it is the truth. If you are ever in Cairo and want a clean bathroom and a dry martini, I can recommend the Cairo Hilton. The Cairo Hilton is in Cairo. One can circum- navigate the globe and have nothing but clean bathrooms and dry martinis simply by staying at Hilton Hotels. Honest.

I cannot and do not recommend the Hanoi Hilton. The Hanoi Hilton is a hoax. Hilton should look into the matter. First, the bathrooms aren't all that clean and the bars don't serve dry martinis. There isn't even a proper bar. Why President Nixon should call a scummy prison the Hanoi Hilton is more than I can understand. Several scholars have suggested he was attempting irony. I am grateful for their help.

The Hanoi Hilton has one great advantage over the Cairo Hilton. The Hanoi Hilton has a proper air raid shelter. When the French were the innkeepers they called their raid shelter a dungeon. The North Vietnamese called the dungeon an air raid shelter. Each night they herded the POWs down into the dungeon, which of course they called the air raid shelter. The only bit of light came from a few clear glass light bulbs hung from braided wire. It was mostly dark and dank and smelled of high school locker rooms and unflushed toilets. It is really quite· shocking, Mr. Hilton.

The dungeon did offer protection against most bombs and the POWs were safe. This made the manager of the Hanoi Hilton happy. The North Vietnamese know a valuable item when they see one. The POWs were the only chip that Mr. Le Dc Tho had to play in his Paris game with Henry Kissinger. Each night the American bombers came. Each night it was down to the dungeon with the POWs. Each night the POWs pissed and moaned at their inconvenience.

"I don't know why the commies won't let us stay in our rooms." It was Rex King, bitching as usual.

"They want to protect us. They've got to. It's in Article

23, League of Nations Accord 1923." That legal opinion was given by Lieutenant Justin Kleinschmidt of the Judge Advocate Generals Corps. Justin Kleinschmidt was the only prisoner contributed by the Judge Advocate Generals Corps. Judge Advocates usually go about drawing up bills of particular against soldiers that go absent without leave or get drunk or insult officers or do any of the things soldiers normally do. Sometimes Judge Advocates just sit around and drink coffee or something stronger. They don't usually get thrown in prison-- their own country's or anyone else's. That could be the reason they like to toss soldiers into the stockade. A stockade is what an army calls a prison for its own soldiers.

Now Justin Kleinschmidt sat in the dungeon of the Hoa Lo Prison. He was captured while performing an everyday act. He was pissing. Soldiers are not ordinarily captured that way. Certainly Judge Advocates are not captured that way in any war, no matter how gross. Justin Kleinschmidt excepted, of course.

"Kleinschmidt you, don't you know that they are brain washing us?" Lieutenant Colonel Rex King lived in fear of being brain washed. He did everything possible to avoid that method of hygiene.

"You can hear the bombs. They are protecting us just like I say." A really nasty stick of bombs fell on Friendship of Nations Road just outside the gray stone walls of the Hanoi Hilton. Happily it was just an ordinary stick of bombs. Air Force Operational Planning (AFOPs) wisely and humanely forbade their bombers from dropping the giant concussion bombs within one kilometer of the Hanoi Hilton. One kilometer is an easy way of saying 0.62 miles. Dungeons offer scant protection from concussion bombs.

Concussion bomb is the straightforward name for a bomb that gives people concussions. AFOPs didn't want to give the POWs a concussion. The POWs were very popular items. AFOPs intelligence reported the prisoners were nightly in the dungeon. The word intelligence when used by the military means finding out what the other side is doing and has nothing to do with intelligence in the usual sense of the word.

No concussion bombs were dropped. AFOPs ordered the Lazy Dog.

AFOPs is a very tough place to work. The hours are long. The Air Force drops bombs at the damnedest hours. To work at AFOPs one must be ambitious, diplomatic and hard working. An understanding wife helps. The AFOPs worker's wife must greet her man with a dry martini and a smile. When the wife asks how the day went, the AFOPS say, "It was a fucking tough day, honey." And a tough day it usually was. A lot of pressure is put on AFOPs. A lot of people want to order bombs dropped. A· lot of people like to drop bombs. The Air Force bombs. The United States Navy bombs. The Marines bomb. Sometimes even the Coast Guard bombs, when they have a chance to drop bombs out of their helicopters. The Army sometimes bombs without even asking AFOPs. It is the responsibility of the folks at AFOPs to co-ordinate all of this bombing. It is bloody hard work. People are always yelling at you to drop bombs. Generals want a say in what kind of bombs should be dropped where. Admirals promote their pet ideas. Civilians at the Pentagon on large salaries are especially fond of offering their thoughts. Bomb makers are always pestering AFOPs to drop more bombs. The White House, that is to say the President, likes to suggest where and when bombs should be dropped. Presidents down the years have seemed to derive pleasure from ordering that such and such a place be bombed with such and such a bomb. Mr. Nixon liked to say: "Drop one of the big ones." It is very hard work at AFOPs, but it gets one ahead and the jobs there are very much in demand. At AFOPs one can say, "Drop a Lazy Dog on Friendship of Nations Road around midnight tonight." And sure enough around midnight down comes a Lazy Dog.

The Lazy Dog is a good deal larger than even a fat apartment bound Saint Bernard. The Lazy Dog explodes a few feet above the ground and spews 200 little puppy-sized bombs called guavas. The pups were named guavas by the wit in the Ordinance Development Section of the Department of Defense

(ODSOTDOD) after the fruit that is yellow on the outside and pink on the inside. ODSOTDOD doesn't really develop any ordinance; they buy it from various companies listed on the New York Stock Exchange. The people that work for ODSOTDOD and the one wit are allowed to think they develop ordinance. It is a small indulgence on the part of the bomb merchants.

The Lazy Dog is warranted by the manufacturer to "kill or maim anyone not in a shelter within a 100 meter radius of impact." One hundred meters is another way of saying 109.36 yards. Impact is another way of saying the place where the thing goes boom. Each guava is packed not only with TNT, but with jagged bits of plastic as well. The plastic is transparent to X-rays.

Sterile conditions are not used in the guava manufacturing process. Lucky POWs to be in the dungeon when the Lazy Dog does his duty.

"You can hear those bombs. Why those boys can drop a bomb in a tin drum on parade day, the things they have now-a-days."

"The fuckers are bombing us, King." Kleinschmidt prided himself on being a realist.

"They are bombing the Commies, not us. AFOPs wouldn't let them. That's not the American way." King has been known to have difficulties with reality.

"So they say," answered Major John H. Sloan. Major Sloan had heard of Peace with Honor, but he didn't believe one word of it.

"Let's hear it for the good old Red, White and Blue. Hats off for our boys, God bless 'em." shouted Lieutenant Colonel Rex King.

"Oh, for Christ sakes, King. King, knock it off." Major Sloan was tired of King's patriotic drivel. It wouldn't be so bad if King felt the least bit bad about his capture. He didn't. King was actually happy. Major Sloan had no real hopes of going home.

If he ever got out, he couldn't be sure things would be much better.

"You're going to get it, Sloan. You're really going to get it."

"I know, I know." Sloan thought that he was going to get it. Get it if he ever got back home. Get it for not doing his best, for getting captured, for being a prisoner of the North Vietnamese. It worried him a lot. He had visions of a court- martial and Leavenworth. The Army prison in Kansas is not a nice place.

"You're going to get it too, King," said Kleinschmidt.

"Just what do you mean by that?"

"You surrendered just like the rest of us," said lawyer Kleinschmidt.

"I was shot down." He was not. He ejected.

"You put up your hands and surrendered just like the rest of us."

"Just you watch it you shave"...'tail."[CHECK THIS]

"A soldier is supposed to fight, not surrender."

"I am not a soldier."

"A parachutist, that's the same thing." Air Force and Navy prisoners were called parachutists by the Army prisoners. The last leg of the parachutists' trip to North Vietnam was by parachute, Navy men included. The Air Force prisoners called the Navy prisoners squids. A squid is a creature that lives in the sea. Sometimes Navy men go to sea. The parachutists and the squids called the Army prisoners grunts. Soldiers, real soldiers of the infantry kind, live an unpleasant life and grunt a lot. Parachutists, squids and grunts called the Marine prisoners jarheads. Marines aren't considered to be very smart, neither are jars. The parachutists, the squids, the grunts and the jarheads called the CIA prisoners spooks. They thought that the

CIA prisoners were spies. As far as I know, there were no Coast Guard prisoners. If one happened to fall out of his helicopter, perhaps he would have been called a high jumper. It is a matter of speculation.

Sergeant Le Roy Kaiser drove an Air Force blue Ford Galaxy 500 toward the Eglin Air Force Base BOQ to collect First Lieutenant Roderick Vincent Wellborne III. The Air Force car did not have a radio that played music. The Department of Defense watches the taxpayers' money with care. Sergeant Kaiser hung his own small Japanese transistor radio the size of a small Japanese transistor radio on the rear view mirror. It played music. It cost $8.79 plus tax.

Sergeant Kaiser and Lieutenant Wellborne have two things in common. Both men are grossly overpaid. Both are premature ejaculators. Other than that they are different in every way. They are from two different worlds--two different galaxies. Le Roy is black; Roderick--white. Le Roy graduated from Booker T. Washington Junior High School, the one in Valdosta, Georgia; Roderick--Yale, the one in New Haven, Connecticut. Le Roy always looked as though he were wearing his trousers sideways; Roderick--tailored. Le Roy has hemorrhoids; Roderick doesn't. Le Roy inherited sickle-cell anemia; Roderick--a patent medicine fortune. Le Roy rubbed Preparation H on his glans in an effort to become a mature ejaculator; Roderick--Nupercainal. And so on.

The First Lieutenant wears the gold aiguillettes of a presidential aide over his left shoulder. People use to get on horses from the left side. He was on an official presidential mission. He was going to escort Mrs. King to the White House.

As the White House was in Republican hands, Roderick Vincent Wellborne III considered himself honored. He thought he was saving the world from Communism. He really did. No fooling.

The Lieutenant Wellborne had had one profound thought in his life. And that thought was a question: "Why is it such a good thing to run the hundred yard dash in ten seconds and it is such a bad thing to fuck in five seconds?"

"Turn that radio off."

"Yes, sir."

"Hell, if you really want to keep it on, do." It was a sunny day in Florida and Lieutenant Wellborne is not all that bad a fellow.

The blue Air Force Galaxy 500 had two bumper stickers sticking to the back bumper. One was authorized by the Air Force itself. It said: SEND HOME OUR POWs. The other was authorized by Lieutenant Colonel Rex King before he ·became a POW, but while he was in charge of the Sedan Section of the Eglin Air Force Base Motor Pool (SSOTEAFBHP). That sticker said: Honk if you love JESUS.

The traffic on the Miracle Strip Parkway was moving like tomato catsup. The Ford Galaxy was stuck in the traffic. The top may as well have been on the bottle. Sergeant Kaiser passed the time wondering whether or not to retire after twenty years service at half pay or wait for thirty years and get two-thirds pay. He didn't know one thing about the actuarial sciences. That didn't stop him from wondering. His hemorrhoids started itching like mad. That stopped him. "Jesus," he said.

The traffic started moving in one big gush. The Ford sat there. The cars behind started honking as if they loved JESUS.

"What the fuck are they honking about?" said Sergeant Le Roy Kaiser.

A Dodge van with foot wide tires sped by, its horn honking. The driver looked like the model for a funeral parlor portrait of Jesus Christ. The van had a mural of the Grand Canyon at sunset painted on its side. The sun was setting in the east. The driver made an obscene gesture. It wasn't Jesus; it was an Air Force general's son. Air Force generals and their sons seem fond of making obscene gestures. There must be some genetic predisposition towards the making of obscene gestures by those that ply the general's trade.

"Up yours," yelled Sergeant Kaiser.

"Hippy," said Lieutenant Wellborne.

A few other cars honked as they passed. Maybe they loved Jesus. Maybe not. Maybe if Le Duc Tho read the bumper sticker he would send home the prisoners. Maybe not. Maybe he would just honk. Maybe not.

Mrs. King was ready. Dressed in her new navy blue pants suit, she was ready to travel. The wig case for two was parked by the front door. The Budweiser cans were still wound round with hair. Her ears, wrists and neck smelled of Joy perfume. She bought the Joy for Rex King's homecoming. She had Jean Patou confused with Doctor Alex Comfort.

Mrs. King pushed the button marked T on her microwave oven. The microwave oven responded with the exact time in neon lights. The manufacturer liked to brag that his oven tells the time with "split-second accuracy." He is right. The oven gives the time with great precision. It also gave the cat cataracts. The micro- waves clouded the beast's eyes like the white of an egg hitting a hot griddle.

Lieutenant Wellborne and Sergeant Kaiser arrived on schedule without the aid of a microwave oven. They made do with something called a Rolex Oyster. Rolex Oyster is the trade name of an ex- pensive Swiss watch. Pity that Sergeant Kaiser's Rolex Oyster was made in Taiwan. He bought it from a nice chap that stood him to a few drinks in a bar in Destin, Florida. The watch got them to Mrs. King's quarters on time.

"Let's get going, buster." Mrs. King is polite only to field grade officers.

"Sergeant, take Mrs. King's suitcase." It was a wig case, but never mind. Sergeant Kaiser took it anyway.

The cat smelling the fresh air made a dash for the front door. The screen door was shut.

"Dumb fucking cat," said Mrs. King.

Lieutenant Wellborne, ignoring the stunned--silly Siamese said, "We had better be on our way, Sergeant. We want to go to Eglin Flight Ops."

Sergeant Kaiser looked at his trip ticket and wanted to say no shit. He said, "Yes, sir."

The catsup flowed freely back to town. No one honked. No one loved Jesus. Down the Miracle Strip Parkway sped the Ford Galaxy 500, past Bacon's By the Sea and Mary Ester. It turned into the back entrance of Eglin Air Force Base and drove out on the 5,000-foot tarmac and squealed to a stop right by the White House Jetstar II. The notation II after the word Jetstar means the craft has four engines. Perhaps Mr. Dan Houghton of the Lockheed Company could explain this apparent contradiction. If he is at a loss, maybe one of his Japanese friends could.

A Filipino steward dressed in a double-breasted white mess jacket stood at the foot of the self-contained stairs of the Lockheed Jetstar II. The jacket had modest epaulettes and on the left breast a small black plastic tag with a single word engraved. That word was: Manolo.

"Welcome to Presidential plane, Missy." Manolo Rivera y El Rey knew how to say miss, but he had been around the White House long enough to know that American ladies or at least American ladies on their way to the White House like to be called Missy by Filipino stewards.

"Is this thing safe?"

"Oh yes, Missy. Boss man himself use it to go to New York one time. He like very much. Very safe, you bet."

"Hell, I'm going to Washington."

"Yes Missy, please come on board."

The inside of the Jetstar II was outfitted as a conference room. A large teak table ran the length of the cabin. Three fake Eames chairs waited on each side. A large swivel chair covered with soft black glove leather crowned the table. Mrs. King sat herself down at the ersatz throne. Lieutenant Wellborne made do with one of the fake Eames. Manolo presented Mrs. King with a royal blue flight bag containing: a blue nylon jacket with the Presidential seal printed in gold on the left breast and under the seal the words Air Force One (the Jetstar II wasn't grand enough to be Air Force One), a pack of stationery, a deck of playing cards with the Presidential seal printed thereon, a sewing kit and a shoe shine kit. The shoeshine kit was put there by Manolo Rivera y El Rey at his own expense. It was his way of saying that he wasn't going to shine any shoes. Someone not in the business of serving travelers on their way to see the President of the United States of America can't possibly imagine how often people want their shoes shined.

The stairs started whirring and up they came. The door swung shut of its own accord. Manolo locked it in place. A green light came on and the pilot did whatever pilots do to make a plane fly.

Down the runway roared the Jetstar II and off into the air, off toward Washington, well really off to Andrews Air Force Base.

"Would you like something to drink, Missy?"

"Yes, a martini."

"I bet I know how Missy like martini, very dry, right Missy?"

"You bet your ass."

A lot of martinis are drunk on White House jets and Manolo keeps them made up well in advance. Soon he would be saying to Mrs. King: "I hope this is dry enough for Missy." Manolo wasn't sure how a martini could be dry or why that term should be used. The closest thing he could figure out was no vermouth meant dry and dry meant good.

"What will you have, sir?"

"I'll have a kier."

"So sorry sir, but this craft equipped only with class B refreshment kit." True enough. The class B refreshment kit (USAFVIPRK Hark IV-Class B) called for several cases of Montrachet and for one bottle of Crème de Cassis, however.

"It is just as well, I have work to do. "

And that was true enough. He pulled a fan fold IBM computer listing from his regulation Air Force brief case. The business was not Air Force business. The business was family business. He was going to pick a likely sounding name for a surgical jelly that can be had in any drug store for 69 cents. The family firm planned to sell the jelly for $4.98, once a suitable name could be found. The name was hidden in the IBM listing. The computer print out came from an IBM J60/40 computer sold to the Air Force by a superior IBM salesman. The figures J60/40 have no meaning. A superior computer salesman is a salesman that sells computers to people who don't need computers. IBM calls their superior computer salesmen account executives. The Air Force and a lot of other people have computers they don't need or they don't know how to use. Lieutenant Wellborne knows how to use a computer. He learned how at a place called The B School, which is in Cambridge, Massachusetts.

The IBM computer used a set of instructions donated by a famous drug company to The B School in exchange for a large tax deduction. The instructions compelled the computer to spew forth masses of likely sounding names for drugs. Student Wellborne stole the program for future use. The future had come and along with the future--free computer time. Thanks to a motivated IBM salesman and the generosity of the American taxpayers, a new word would be available for small boys to snicker at. That word was hidden in the IBM printing. Unhappily it was hidden toward the end of the list. IBM machines print things in alphabetical order and it would take young Wellborne the better part of the trip to find the magic name.

Abiosan, Abiosen, Abiosin, Abiotic.

Manolo put the martini down on a coaster saying: White House Air Force. Beside that he placed a miniature ice bucket with a carafe full of dry martini peeking out. It was the same sort of carafe that one finds in St. Louis. There were paper napkins printed:

Stolen from a wing of the White House.

Not the East Wing.

Not the West Wing.

But, the Air Wing.

The jet raced toward Andrews Air Force Base at close to the speed of sound. Mrs. King drank dry martinis. The plane arrived safely. Mrs. King arrived a bit tight. Lieutenant Wellborne arrived with the name that would allow him and his heirs to live in abject luxury most of the time and on Martha's Vineyard the rest of the time.

That name was: VAGILUBE.

Mrs. King said, "Missy would like one more martini, thank you."

All air traffic in and out of Andrews Air Force Base halted as the small presidential jet came in from Florida. The Jetstar II touched down easily and braked slowly, taking the entire runway to come to a full stop--such was the pilot's consideration for his passenger.

Another presidential aide helicoptered in to meet Mrs. King. He was a Naval man. Presidents fancy Naval men as aides. In times gone by, Naval officers went to sea, and for long times at that. They know proper respect for the captain and they set a wonderful table. An Army man, if not actually dirty, looked too clean. Even a president could tell that a Marine was out of touch. The Air Force is much too new to have any tradition. A Navy man makes the better aide. Let there be no doubt about that.

The Naval officer, who was from Kansas, boarded the plane; the starboard engines stopped whining. He greeted Mrs. King and said to Lieutenant Wellborne, "I'll escort Mrs. King to the White House."

"But--"

"Wait here, Lieutenant." Little did the Navy man know that Wellborne would soon squeeze him out of his plush job. If he had, perhaps he wouldn't have been so rude.

Close by waited a giant Navy blue and white helicopter painted with the Seal of the President of the United States of America and an American Flag facing in the wrong direction.

Under the Seal in Helvetica type were the words: United States of America.

Before Regina King could eat her last olive, the Navy man had her off the Jetstar II and on to the garish helicopter. The helicopter was furnished like an admiral's gig--all white canvas, Turks Heads, money fists, man rope knots, tassels, the lot.

The helicopter trip would thrill a Buddhist monk. There, spread below, is L'Enfant's Washington--a giant star fish. The Capitol, the monument, the mall, the small flame at Arlington pass below. The noise, the smell of white canvas and the descent to the east lawn of the White House conspire to make one giddy.

The doorway of the helicopter was designed for midgets. It caught and skewed Mrs. King's beehive wig. Future Presidents would bump their heads on that very transom to the great delight of many photographers.

The whole thing was a " too much for a middle-aged lady to take. The excitement of leaving on such short notice caused her to forget her girdle, so instead of looking like a firm fat lady she looked like a blubbery fat lady. That slip of memory, the helicopter trip, the wig, the martinis and the Western love of emaciation and youth would cause the President of the United States Mr. Richard M. Nixon to leave the White House over Christmastide.

Never did the White House look so nice at Christmas. A twenty-foot plastic Scots pine brushed the ceiling of the blue room. The tree was hung with blue and gold Christmas balls, some of them larger than Mrs. King's wig. The special Christmas balls especially made in Kaiserslautern bore the Presidential seal. Thousands upon thousands of tiny lights twinkled on and off. The lights are known in the trade as firefly lights.

Around and around the great plastic pine tree rested a web of fiberglass spun by Owens-Corning. The tree looked like Los Angeles when viewed from the air during a smog alert.

Ah, but the tree was in good taste compared to the rest of that historic house. Everywhere Mrs. King looked, she saw wreaths and garlands and piles of artificial fruit and plastic pinecones and red satin-like bows. The plastic pinecones were in Mrs. Nixon's own words, "my little contribution."

A machine called Constant Fresh Missed a whiff of aerosol mist every fifteen minutes, twenty-four hours a day, seven days a week. It was run by electricity. The fragrance was called Pine Glade. The blue room smelled like the men's room at Grand Central Station. Some of the aerosol mist condensed on Peale's portrait of George Washington. The father of the country looked like he had been kissing a toad. He smelled like a urinal.

There was not a nook, not a cranny, not a window, not a door, not a wall, not a bathroom, not an office, not a hall, not a stairway, not a bedroom that wasn't decked with some sort of plastic Christmas symbol. There was plastic mistletoe in John Ehrlichman's office and plastic holly in H. R. "Bob" Haldeman's office and plastic poinsettias in the oval office. There was nothing, not one thing that needed watering. Still it grew. It must have been alive and reproducing itself, mutating, spreading from room to room contaminating, drowning everything as it went.

It was as if there was a great plastic cancer growing in the White House that Christmas of 1972.

The White House was the grandest thing Mrs. King or Mr. Nixon or Mrs. Nixon had ever seen. Mr. and Mrs. Nixon had seen the Great Wall and the Great Hall in Peking. No department store looked as lovely. The White House was gaudier than Saks, grosser than Neiman Marcus, tawdrier than Macy's and as vulgar as its namesake Maison Blanche. The family Nixon liked it a lot. Mrs. King liked it more than a lot.

The aide-de-camp, ordered by Ike Tapem to bring Mrs. King to the oval office, brought her there. It was the last official order that Ike Tapem would ever give. He would soon be sacked.

Alexander Butterfield's annunciator board said that the President was in the hide-a-way office in the Executive Office Building across the alley from the White House. The alley is grandly called West Executive Avenue. Sure enough, just as Admiral Butterfield's son's machine had promised, the President sat in his office in the Executive Office Building. The Executive Office Building is known both inside and outside the trade as the EOB. The President was talking to the Very Reverend Francis X. McNaughton, S. J. Father McNaughton was dressed in mufti. His shirt was brand new, but it had someone else's initials on the pocket. The initials were Y. St.L. Father McNaughton knew no one with those initials nor why his shirt should be so marked. Mr. Nixon was dressed like he was going to try for a loan. A tiny enamel flag flew from his left lapel. It had six stars and nine stripes.

The President was going through what was known in the inner circles of the White House as his place in history phase that Christmas. It made life hell for poor Ziegler, Haig, Haldeman, Colson and Ehrlichman. Father McNaughton had been called in to relieve the front line troops. Father McNaughton was now listening to Mr. Nixon say for the third time, "The problem was (is) how to promise significant change in the forthcoming second term, without suggesting that our first term was a failure. I've been in this business too long for this President to admit such a thing, because it would be wrong, that's for sure."

The Very Reverend didn't have to strain his fine Jesuit education to say, "It is a problem much like Benjamin Disraeli's when he succeeded William Gladstone." Haldeman didn't get to be the major domo by letting fools waste the President's time. Father McNaughton was earning his salary.

"Disraeli, that is it, by God. This President is a modern Disraeli."

Father McNaughton didn't feel that it was his place to tell the President that Disraeli was a hopeless womanizer, an old Jew who wore rouge and a wig and was altogether a foolish and vain old man. Father McNaughton was about to make a small joke about a Gladstone bag, when Mrs. King traipsed past the open door of the EOB office.

"Jesus Christ, what the fuck is a circus fat lady doing in the EOB?" Thus spoke the President of the United States of America.

The Very Reverend Francis X. McNaughton S. J.'s back faced the door. He didn't have a clue why the President should shift from Disraeli to the circus. He stared blankly.

Rose Mary Wood buzzed and told the Chief of State he was wanted in the oval office for some photo opportunities. What the fuck, thought the President. It can't be worse than talking to this dumb jebby.

The light on Mr.Butterfield's annunciator board shifted from EOB to Oval.

The aide-de-camp trotted Mrs. King across West Executive Avenue toward the side entrance of the West Wing of the White House. As she trotted the cheeks of her ass proved Newton's First Law. A body in motion tends to remain in motion. When her left leg advanced her huge left ham went up and as her left leg came down, the ham continued skyward until the downward vector overcame the upward mass. Left ham up, boom. Left ham down, pooff. Right ham up, boom. Right ham down, pooff. Every sixth cycle the two hams went up in close harmony. It was a lesson in wave theory.

She puffed, puffed and wheezed, boomed and pooffed. Mrs. King's pink face turned from her usual pale pink to pinker pink to archbishop red. The martinis were about to do her in.

H. L. "Bob" Haldeman said a single word, "Ziegler."

"Yeah," said the President.

Enter Ron Ziegler, followed by Regina King, the fat lady. Tapem waited outside the oval office and strained to listen. He puffed

on a menthol cigarette, the last he would smoke at 1600·
Pennsylvania Avenue.

"Hi, Ron," said the President.

 "Yeah, I just wanted to check. Are we ready to go? "

"Jesus, who is that?" The President whispered so only Ziegler
could understand. I don't think Mrs. King heard. Nixon nudged
Ziegler. Ziegler winced.

"Regina King, the POW wife." The currency of manners is not
held in high regard by the White House staff.

"Sit down, sit down. This..."

Gooseflesh broke out to the extent gooseflesh can break out on
a very fat lady. The sweat poured from both armpits. The stick
anti-perspirant didn't work at all. The smell of sweat masked
the smell of the Joy and the gin. She was cardinal red. Her
blood pressure was 240/180. The figures 240 and 180 have
something to do with millimeters of mercury and are very
important figures. She tried to speak. She couldn't. The gin
wouldn't let her. She was still puffing.

The President looked uncomfortable. He knew and had
overcome the curse of haphazard sweat. He thought why in the
name of God doesn't she use some kind of deodorant.

Sometimes gin comes to the rescue. The gin came to the rescue
and Mrs. King panted, "Oh thank you Mr. President Nixon.

"I am really thrilled and don't know what to say."

"The President is, well frankly proud of what your husband did,
has done. No one was, has stood taller--by that, I mean
prouder--than your brave husband." Mr. Nixon didn't know
who Rex King was, much less the details of his ejection and
capture.

"We are all so proud of Rex." She was proud of Rex.

"Yeah, never before has this great nation been so well served by its POWs."

Mrs. King inflated with pride and asked the President of the United States of America, "When are they going to let our husbands come home?"

Then she hiccupped.

"Well now, we are bombing them (the North Vietnamese) like they've never been bombed before. Night and day. There will be nothing left to bomb, except for your brave husband and of course the other POWs, fine men every one of them. Scowcroft says that wouldn't do much good anyway. Bad for images. AFOPs says there is nothing left to bomb. And frankly I might say that the North Vietnamese are not far removed from savages. And let me tell you that I know something about, not everything mind you, but something about Communism. Ah, where did you say you were from?"

"Florida, Mr. President." Mrs. King hiccupped one more time. "Do you know Don Shula?"

"Ah..." Mrs. King wondered if she had had too much to drink. She had. Another hiccup sounded.

"Are you ready for the photographers, Mr. President?" It was Ron Ziegler speaking.

"Yeah," said the President as he came to his feet. "Now if you will excuse me Mrs. er—ah..."

"Mrs. King is the photo opportunity. She is the only POW wife we could come up with. It seems that the rest of 'em are in Los Angeles or somewhere like that."

"Los Angeles," said Mrs. King. That cured the hiccups. "Right," said the President for reasons known only to himself.

"Shall I let them come in or do you want to make up first?"

"Ah..." The President wanted out. The last thing, the very last thing he wanted was to have his picture taken with a tipsy fat lady. He wanted to say: "Get her out of here. The politician in him wouldn't let him. She might be a voter.

Nixon always said, "Never piss off a voter."

He lived by that code. That code caused his blood pressure to peak at 190/150. That is an important figure.

The photographer was waiting and listening just outside the door of the oval office. Tapem and the photograp_her made little comments during Mrs. King's audience. The photograp_her had a brand new Hasselblad. A Hasselblad is an expensive Swedish camera. He had paid a good deal more for it than he could possibly afford. He was just the Saturday photographer. He had bought the Hasselblad on time in the hopes of selling a few pictures on the sly to one of the movie magazines or maybe even Playboy. Photographer to the President is a position of trust.

"Well, Mrs. er—ah..."

"King," said Ziegler.

"King," said Mr. Nixon as he walked out of the room. Ziegler followed close at heel.

A secret service man entered the oval office. No one is ever left alone in the oval office except the President himself or one of the cleaning ladies.

The President shouted at Ziegler, "Goddanm it, I'm not going to have my picture taken with any asshole of a circus fat lady, that's for sure."

"But, Mr. President."

"Listen you dumb fuck, I thought the POWs up, they're mine. Mine, goddamn it, mine."

Mr. Nixon didn't think the POWs up. Some of them were there long before Mr. Nixon came to power. Mr. Nixon didn't even think up the idea of making the POWs into heroes. That is what he meant. George Nickleman conceived and nurtured the hero image. Richard Nixon seldom gave Nickleman credit for any of his brilliant notions. We'll meet George Nickleman later. Now back to Mr. Nixon.

"They are mine I tell you. This President will not ruin the POW image by posing with a whale. Now get her out of here, don't argue."

"Hell, I'm not arguing. Again, you see, can't argue. I'm just passing this point to you." A press secretary has to be good with words. The photographer fondly fondled his new Hasselblad. He looked worried. He was worried that he would miss the chance of taking some pictures. He thought, then said, "Maybe we could get Kissinger. If we put him on the left side of the President and the fat dame on the right side, it would sort of balance things out. It would make a fine picture, it really would."

"Well, it's no deal. I will not ruin the POW image with a single picture." The President was speaking with great moral indignation, like an honest judge when offered a bribe.

Ike Tapem looked like he was going to pee in his pants. He pulled his jacket tight across his chest in an effort to hide the coffee stains. His shoes fit badly and he shifted his weight from foot to foot. His nose itched.

The President goes for the neck. "Who brought her here? You, you, whoever you are. You did it. You look like the one. What the fuck's your name--name?"

"Tapem," said Tapem. He wet the floor. He had his best suit on. It was a tan suit.

"You bastard. You bastard. Have the secret service get him out of here. He is an enemy. Get'm, get him out now." The President screamed, "Secret service." He couldn't have screamed louder if the whole Baader-Meinhof gang had been spraying the place with a machine gun.

The secret service man with Mrs. King leaped like a lumberjack hearing the dinner bell. He was at the President's side before the President stopped his stuttering shout. Tapem was out of the White House and onto Pennsylvania Avenue in less time than it takes Sergeant Le Roy Kaiser to fuck-—Preparation H or no Preparation H.

"I will not have my picture taken with her." The President was still shouting, not quite as loud, but still shouting.

Mrs. King heard it all.

Mrs. King looked around the oval office. There were plastic poinsettias, a crackling fire in a real fireplace, two sofas, two flags, the Great Seal embedded in the carpet; there were no women. There was nothing that could be called a her.

Mrs. King realized Mr. Nixon, the President of the United States of America, was talking about her. She was the circus fat lady. She was the one the President wouldn't have his picture taken with. She was the one the President wanted the fuck out of the oval office.

It is no fun being fat. It is no fun being married to one of the very few pilots in the entire United States Air Force who doesn't drink. It is no fun being married to a pilot who thinks he is a preacher. She was used to all this and could take it very well. She could take having her husband a prisoner in Hanoi, indeed it gave her some status she would not otherwise have. She could take her lonely sexless life. She could not take leaving Florida on such short notice at the direction of one of the President's flunkies, only to have the President himself call her an asshole of a circus fat lady.

Tears filled her eyes. Her nostrils flared like a cow's when ready for bull. Her nose began to run. Her giant bosom shook and the tears came like a summer's storm.

The President heard it all. He cannot abide crying women be they fat or be they thin. He said to no one, "I'm going to Florida to see Bebe."

Mrs. King's vast body heaved with sobs and she wept uncontrollably.

The President stormed out of the anteroom with Ziegler close behind. The secret service men joined in the chase. The photographer wished for some daylight film or at least for some sun filters. General Haig called out, "What about the dispatch cases?"

"Send them on the Jetstar, have Dean bring them." Mr. Nixon trusted John Dean.

The President jogged to the east lawn and flew off in the helicopter that had been waiting for Mrs. King.

An hour later, the Presidential dispatch cases, Roderick Vincent Wellborne III and Manolo Rivera y El Rey would fly the Jetstar II to Florida.

The only people who knew why Mrs. King was in the oval office were on their way to Florida or out on Pennsylvania Avenue looking through the iron fence. Ike Tapem held tightly to the iron fence. He was cold and the freezing urine helped not one bit. He said out loud, "I'll fix the asshole, I really will."

Mrs. King was left alone in the oval office. Her sobs were recorded for some future historian. When the cleaning women came in they found her sobbing still.

Most of Hanoi had been bombed flat. Le Duc Tho's villa was bombed flat. It was just a four-room house with a cook shed out back. The cook shed was bombed flat. Le Duc Tho called his house a villa; even a Communist has his vanity. Le Duc Tho got in the habit of calling his house a villa when dealing with Dr. Henry Kissinger in Paris.

Dr. Kissinger often talked about his villa in Georgetown. Dr. Kissinger is not the sort of doctor that can take out a gall bladder or prescribe diazepam, but he called himself a doctor nonetheless. Dr. Kissinger called his villa, "My house in Georgetown." The word villa comes from the Latin word vicus--row of houses. Houses in Georgetown come in rows.

Poor Le Du Tho had no place to stay. Rooms were hard to come by in Hanoi that Christmas of 1972. He pulled more than a few strings and booked himself and Mrs. Le Duc Tho a room in the old Imperial Hotel. The Imperial Hotel is now called The Peoples Hotel. The Peoples Hotel is on Friendship of Nations Road, which you will remember as the old Avenue Louis Napoleon. The only people that could stay in The Peoples Hotel were government officials, mainly foreign, or journalists--all foreign.

"I don't know how we can afford this room, Tho." Mrs. Le Duc Tho nagged a lot.

"I don't know what else we can do. Maybe you can go stay with your mother."

"I can't do that. You know how mother is."

"Maybe I can talk them into letting you go back to Paris with me." Name me one wife, just one wife that wouldn't want to go to Paris.

"You don't understand what I'm saying at all, do you?"

"Ah..."

"I thought you said peace was at hand."

"Those were Dr. Kissinger's words."

"You said you wouldn't have to spend so much time in Paris. Besides Paris is so expensive. Where will we find the money? We just have to get a new house and then there is the new furniture. Everything is so dear now-a-days. I don't know how we will do it on what they pay you."

"I make a good salary."

"I bet Mrs. Kissinger doesn't darn his socks."

"The capitalists are corrupt."

"I thought you said that you liked Dr. Kissinger."

"He has his good points."

"Good points? Honestly Tho."

"He does seem friendly."

"Good points? Friendly? He bombed our villa."

"I doubt that he really meant to."

"You said peace negotiations were all wrapped up. Then they go and bomb our villa. I don't think you know what you are doing."

"What experience do you have in peace negotiations? Mother was right."

"Maybe you should have married that dentist."

"At least Dr. Kissinger will have something to do once the peace treaty is signed. "

"He is not a dentist."

"Well, he looks like one."

"He is not."

"Hell, I bet he makes a good living anyway. I've seen his car."

"It is not his, now go to sleep. "

"Sleep? How can I sleep with all those bombs? Just tell me how I can sleep with all those airplanes and all those bombs dropping."

"They are not going to bomb the Imperial, I mean The Peoples Hotel. It is sacrosanct. "The Peoples Hotel was in the diplomatic quarter and just down Friendship of Nations Road from the Hanoi Hilton.

"Sacrosanct, sacrosanct, what kind of a word is that?"

"It means that Dr. Kissinger will not bomb us. There are too many foreigners staying here. You've heard them at breakfast. They won't bomb the old Imperial."

"You said that the bombing was over. Just look at our villa."

"That's different. "

"Different, different, honestly Tho!"

"Go to sleep."

Mrs. Le Duc Tho turned on the bed lamp and picked up her novel. The blackout curtains were drawn. The room smelled of moldy carpet. Le Duc Tho pulled the pillow over his head and tried to get some sleep.

Down in the dungeon, the clear glass light bulbs flickered, dimmed to a pale orange and went out.

"Fucking Commies can't even run an electric company." Rex King bitched about almost everything.

"Fucking hotel," said Mrs. Le Duc Tho. Mr. Le Due Tho was playing opossum and Mrs. Le Duc Tho thought him asleep. She also thought for what they were paying for their hotel room, the very least they could expect was electric lights. The Peoples Hotel was the closest thing Hanoi had to a luxury hotel.

"Fucking Allis-Chalmers," said Pohn Van Ngo, Jr. Pohn Van Ngo, Jr. was in charge of the Allis-Chalmers generator supplying the Hanoi Hilton, The Peoples Hotel and the Bac Mi Hospital with electricity. It was hard work, but a very good job and it kept Mr. Pohn Van Ngo, Jr. away from the front. If he could keep the Allis-Chalmers running, he could keep from fighting. Mr. Pohn Van Ngo, Jr. had a pretty wife, at least he thought her pretty. He had two fine children and Mrs. Pohn Van Ngo, Jr. was expecting another child right after the first of the year. Ngo just loved children and he looked forward to his days off so that he might be with them. He was happy they would soon have another child. He arranged for the delivery to take place in the Bac Mi Hospital. He was proud that he would supply the electricity for the birth.

Both the Hanoi Light and Power Company's power plants had been bombed flat some years ago. What power there was, was supplied by a few auxiliary generators. The bombed-flat sites of the power plants were bombed every few weeks. No one at the offices of the Hanoi Light and Power Company could figure this out. They were somewhat amused that the Americans would waste so much time, money and bombs on the long bombed-flat power plants. There wasn't much left worth bombing, even if you are an American.

Here is why the bombed out power plants were bombed and rebombed. Every few weeks someone at the Pentagon or someone at the White House or some general or some blackmailing admiral would look at a map of Hanoi and see the little symbols for the two power plants and say: "Let's bomb those power plants."

The good folks at AFOPs would say, "Sure."

And the place where the old power plants used to be would be bombed one more time. This had been going on for years.

There was darkness all around. Pohn Van Ngo, Jr. couldn't find his flashlight and lit one candle in the darkness and tried to read his copy of Trouble Shooting the Allis-Chalmers 12-Cylinder Diesel. Ngo had learned English especially to read this one book.

"Ascertain if, ascertain if, I wonder what that means," said Pohn Van Ngo, Jr. out loud to himself.

"I'm scared," said Little Lamar Butte. He was scared. Private Lamar Butte was one of Robert McNamara's "1188's."

An "1188" is a substandard soldier, which of course makes him a sub-standard person. As Army recruitment and draft quotas became harder to meet, Secretary of Defense Robert S. McNamara lowered the Army's mental and physical standards so that the weeds could be killed off along with the flowers. The weeds bore the good Secretary McNamara's name and the Army's directive number "1188." Lest there be any misunderstanding, Mr. McNamara is a man even though he was called a secretary.

Private Lamar Butte was dumb beyond the low standards of the Army directive number "1188." He is white and the Army recruiting sergeant bent the rules more than a little, and now Little Lamar was enjoying the hospitality of the Hanoi Hilton.

"Gentlemen, we are prisoners in a Godless Communistic country that can't even supply us with lights. Join me while I lead us in prayer and remind God that we represent the free enterprise system. Now bow your heads and join me in prayer: Oh God..."

"For Christ sakes, knock it off, King. I am an agnostic." Justin Kleinschmidt wasn't going to take any more of King's prayers and foolishment.

"Oh Lord, forgive this dope-smoking Red, for he knows not of what he says."

"nonce upon a time, and a very good time it was, there was this moocow coming down along the road and this moocow that was coming down along the road meets a nicens little boy named baby tuckoo..."

"Excuse me, God. Kleinschmidt, you're going to get it,....you-- you Shavetail son-of-a-bitch. "

"--"

"And what did moocow say when he meets baby tuckoo?" Little Lamar was intrigued by the story.

The Allis Chalmers 12-cylinder diesel is almost as big as a railroad caboose. Indeed when it left Detroit in 1928 it had been painted red, caboose red. The Allis-Chalmers had been bought by the Department of War for the Army of the Philippines. The Department of War legally changed its name to the Department of Defense in 1947. The nature of their work stayed much the same.

The Army painted the Allis-Chalmers olive drab. If you ever meet a drab olive, don't eat it. The Allis-Chalmers provided all of the power for Camp Clark. In 1942 the Japanese seized the diesel as a prize of war and sent it to Sasebo. There they painted it white. White, as the Japanese found out, was not the best color for an Allis-Chalmers 12-cylinder diesel. It did look smart, like an odd colored fire engine. And like odd colored fire engines it required a lot of cleaning and polishing.

After the war, World War number two, the United States Marines took the Allis-Chalmers 12-cylinder diesel with them when they left for China. When they got to Tsingtao, which is on Kiao-chow Bay, they painted it olive drab. The Marines had to leave China in a bit of a rush in 1948 and they forgot to take the Allis-Chalmers 12-cylinder diesel.

In 1966 after both of the Hanoi Light and Power Company's power plants were bombed flat, the Allis-Chalmers was painted red again and sent to Hanoi as a gift to the people of Hanoi from the people of China.

There is a brass sign welded to the engine block saying in Mandarin, Vietnamese and in French: A gift of the People (citizens?) of China to the Citizens (people?) of Hanoi--1966 (translation mine).

The Allis-Chalmers was a grand sounding thing despite its one cracked cylinder. The timing chain and the valve lifters were exposed for oiling. The timing chain went whirr in a very business like fashion. The valve lifters went clickety-clack in the manner of a Swiss train. Very precise--clickety clack, clickety clack. Pohn Van Ngo, Jr. oiled the valve lifters every 5 minutes and the timing chain every 10 minutes. The spout on the oiling can stretched close to two feet. It had the neck of a crane. In between oil lines mopped off the spilled oil and checked the three gauges. Once each day he polished the brass fittings and the sign the Chinese welded to the engine in the middle of the exercise yard of the Hanoi Hilton. At one end of the sand bag house was an opening to let people in and out and to let fresh air in. A small opening at the other end let the hot air from the radiator out. The diesel made lots of heat. The huge diesel oil tank was buried underground lest it be hit by American bombs and start a fire.

Pohn Van Ngo, Jr. was having little luck with his copy of Trouble Shooting the Allis-Chalmers 12-cylinder Diesel and said, "Fuck it. I'll try cleaning the fuel filter." He cleaned the fuel filter. You have never seen such a mess. The filter was clogged tight with low petroleum distillates (LPDs). Ngo cleaned the filter with great care and started the huge machine. This Allis-Chalmers 12-cylinder diesel had a 1946 Chevrolet 6 cylinder overhead valve gasoline engine as a starting engine.

The Marines put it there. The Allis-Chalmers started clanging and whirring and clickety clacking. Electricity started going down the wires in whatever way electricity goes down wires and the lights came on as a result." Ah, ascertain if must mean the LPDs are gumming up the fuel filter." Those, by the way, were the last words Pohn Van Ngo, Jr. would ever say on this earth.

"If you are not going to read, please turn out the light," said Le Duc Tho.

"Just as I was getting some shut-eye, the Commie bastards turn the lights on. The yellow fuckers have no respect."

Nothing pleased Lieutenant Colonel Rex King.

"Tell me more about baby tuckoo." Little Lamar was ever so fond of stories.

"He was a nicen little boy, " said Lieutenant Justin Kleinschmidt.

"Knock it off about fucking baby fuck who. Who needs it?" asked Parachutist King.

"Little Lamar," answered Major John H. Sloan.

Sloan felt sorry for Little Lamar. Little Lamar was too dumb to last it out in Leavenworth, but sure enough that is where Little

Lamar would go, along with himself, Kleinschmidt and a few of the parachutists.

Sloan knew the details of Little Lamar's capture. He was sure to get it when he got back.

Sloan knew the details of his own capture. He knew he would get time in Leavenworth.

"What did moocow say when he meet baby tuckoo? "

"Moo."

"What did baby tuckoo say?"

Little Lamar was enchanted.

Just then a late wave of B52s came over. B-52 is the name of a large class of bombers. These bombers came all the way from Guam just to bomb Hanoi. Guam is eight hours flying time away. You really have to be keen on bombing to travel that long in a B-52 bomber. The bombers were late. They were late because the microwave oven in the officers club wouldn't make any microwaves.

While the pilots and bombardiers waited for the food to thaw, they drank a good deal more martinis than is good for them. Quite a number of them took along some martinis for the road.

One bombardier, a man from Valdosta, Georgia, joked, "You can't fly on one wing, ha, ha."

They were lucky to find Hanoi.

The drunken bombardier dropped a lazy dog right on the Hanoi Hilton.

AFOPs expressly forbade this. The bombardier did it anyway. He said, "Bombs away."

The bomb went boom and the guavas bounced all over the exercise yard of the Hanoi Hilton. One of the guavas found its way into the sand bag engine house.

It went off. Then there was no one to oil the valve lifters and the timing chain. The timing chain went first with the sound of a fork in a garbage disposal.

The lights went out at the Hanoi Hilton, The Peoples Hotel and at the Bac Mi Hospital.

Mrs. Pohn Van Ngo, Jr. went into premature labor when she heard the news about Mr. Pohn Van Ngo, Jr. By the time she reached the Bac Mi Hospital it had been bombed flat by the drunken American flyers. They thought they were bombing one of Hanoi Light and Power's power plants. The baby died.

"Welcome to Los Angeles, little lady." Dick Westcott wore a condominium salesman's smile. And like a condominium salesman, he had little reason to smile. The Association of POW Wives and Families was about to disappear. The POWs were corning home. They would be on their way once Henry Kissinger stopped his recalcitrant ways toward Le Duc Tho. Dick Westcott was glad in principle that Le Duc Tho was to send home the POWs, but that act would put him out of a job. He worried about the future.

And well he should. He was fifty-five, overweight and in debt. He had spent the night with a $200 a night call girl who needed an episiotomy repair. Still he smiled. He could have passed for a dermatologist counting up the day's take.

"Why, thank you." It was Karen Schuster, the 586th official attendee at the official meeting of the Association of POW Wives and Families. She was not a wife. She was not a family member. She had lived briefly with Justin Kleinschmidt, but that was years ago when they were both going to some law school in New Haven.

She hardly remembered him. Miss Schuster traveled to Los Angeles to protect her virtue. Lawyers seldom worry about virtue, but virtue protection brought her from New York to Los Angeles. Honest Indian.

"You must be proud of Captain Kleinschmidt."

"Who?"

"Captain Kleinschmidt, your young man, now."

"You must be very proud of him."

Westcott was repeating himself. His smile was now more of undertakers when using the trocar.

"Uh, yeah."

"Well, we have a Family Assistance Officer along in a few minutes." The trocar smile left Dick Westcott's face. He had spent his life raising money for good causes and raising money for good causes sharpens the senses. He knows when things aren't going his way. The color of his skin matched the green of his double knit suit. It could have been because of last night's gin. He smelled of last night's gin, musk oil and stale K-Y jelly. He had cut himself shaving. A small bit of toilet paper stuck to the wound.

Dick Westcott worked the ad hoc charity field. In his youth he had thought there was more to be made in disasters than in orphans, disease and the poor. Usually he worked floods in India, droughts in Dahomey and earthquakes in Ecuador--slim pickings as it turned out. He was lucky to break even. He was getting old and deals like the POWs don't come along that often. His destiny was tied to the man behind many a good cause, George Nickleman. If George Nickleman said be nice to Karen Schuster; then nice to her he would be.

You will remember George Nickleman as the man that thought up the POWs for Mr. Nixon. He thought up the Association of POW Wives and Families for Dick Westcott. And let me tell you that Dick Westcott showed his gratitude. He was grateful. The Association of POW Wives and Families was his best venture ever. It was a sweet deal as they say in the fund raising business. Money was easy to raise. The money came in by itself and there was really nothing to spend it on. The Texans and the CIA provided any of the airplanes needed from time to time. The Pentagon, that is to say the American taxpayers, paid all the expenses for the meetings. The sales of bumper stickers and bracelets more than covered the expense of running the office. The bracelets were of cupro-nickel and were very popular items. Millions of Americans wore them. Each bracelet had a POWs name engraved on it along with the POWs date of capture. The owners of the bracelets spoke of the man whose name it was as "my POW."

Dick Westcott never dared to dream of such a good cause. It would be a long time before another deal like the POWs along. The POWs were certain to replace the Yangtze River floods as the sweet deal of the century. Whenever the old timers, the fund raiser of yore, got together, the Yangtze River floods, with all those millions of homeless, starving Chinese, always came up. The floods were discussed with affection only a fundraiser could appreciate. How the money poured in. It came, as some of the old timers liked to joke, in floods. The POWs were better than any old Yangtze River flood and there weren't all those starving, homeless bleeding Chinese siphoning off the gravy.

It now looked as if the POWs were coming home at last. Dick Westcott was looking around, as they say. Westcott had been in the business long enough to know when a deal is over it is over. Dick Westcott had spent the last four years working the POWs. During those years he missed out on a first rate tidal wave in Pakistan, two major earthquakes, one in Iran and the other in that wonderful place Managua, Nicaragua--it came at Christmas, talk about your sweet deals--not to mention losing out on a really good famine in Bangladesh. Westcott hated to miss out on a famine. "Fucking POWs," he would say whenever he heard of a famine or earthquake. Now that the POW's were coming home, he checked world rainfall every day. Droughts make for the best famines. Locusts are very undependable.

If Dick Westcott had it to do over again he would go into heart or cancer, good solid professions both of them. He was condemned to trading in the whims of nature, war, politicians, engineers and George Nickleman. After a few gins, when his regret over not going into cancer is at its worst, he cheers himself by thinking of his chums that went into polio. They are walking the street looking for a new disease. Fat chance. All the good diseases had long since been bagged. Only a few unpronounceable diseases are still kicking around. Who would want to give money to a disease he can't even pronounce? Nobody. Dick Westcott would think of this as he pulls on his gin and gives secret toasts to Ho Chi Minh.

"A family what?"

"A Family Assistance Officer." Dick Westcott needed a drink. He had become a morning drinker of late.

"Oh, I don't need that, I'm on the pill. Say what the fuck is going on here anyway?" Karen Schuster always said exactly what she thought. Saying exactly what one thinks is incompatible with making a good living in the legal trade.

Karen Schuster worked for a Wall Street law firm that wasn't on Wall Street, but on Park Avenue. She hadn't advanced past junior associate, but she was with a fine firm. A fine firm is one that makes lots of money. New Haven, not her frankness, got her there. Better, if angling for one of the fine firms, is the law school in Cambridge. New Haven is not a bad second choice.

Miss Schuster was from Great Neck. Great Neck is a place on Long Island and is not meant to be a description of her. She was indistinguishable from all the other girls from Great Neck until she went to Barnard where she became indistinguishable from all the other girls at Barnard. W.H. Auden was at Columbia and Bob Pack at Barnard and she read poetry. Miss Schuster drank at the West End Bar on Broadway and ate at the Shanghai on Saturday nights. In her senior year she met Justin Kleinschmidt and applied for a place in the Yale Law School. Kleinschmidt went his way and Miss Schuster entertained various Sterling Professors.

She was pretty. Let there be no doubt about that. She boasted good eyes, fine bones and a nose sculptured. Her nose was in fact sculptured. The term used for the sculpturing of noses is the same one used for the neutering of cats--fixed. Her nose was fixed by a plastic surgeon with offices on Park Avenue. The surgeon was not made of plastic, nor was her nose. The nose was pretty, upturned, like one of those draw-me pictures one used to see on the back of match covers.

Karen had what is known as good tits, by those who care about such things. Good tits means big tits. Miss Schuster had big tits. They sagged ever so slightly. Her nipples were larger than an Eisenhower silver dollar. An Eisenhower silver dollar is made of cupro-nickel.

Like many a pretty girl that lives and works in the great cities of the world, Karen always looked well turned out. She spent a good deal of time and money on her clothes. She was styled in New York. If her breasts weren't tired, she didn't wear a brassiere. Each year her breasts sagged just a little bit n1ore and the Eisenhower silver dollar spread ever so slightly from the weight.

Even if she hadn't needed it, this bralessness attracted many a horny man. She knew this and rather liked it. She did wonder why so many men looked slightly cross-eyed. Looking at nipples while trying to avoid looking like one is looking at nipples tends to make one look cross-eyed. Many a partner on Park Avenue looked cross-eyed from time to time

Law partners, the Wall Street kind in particular, use the wiles of a Moroccan rug dealer. Rather than mint tea in the back room, it is martinis at the Cote Basque. Instead of smooth-skinned young boys, Karen's firm distracted the clients with Karen. Nothing like a cross-eyed client, the partners thought. That is not to say that the partners wanted Karen to go to bed with any of the clients. Indeed one or two would blanch at the suggestion. Still, they distracted the clients with her very now and again. Oh, I should point out that a client is what you and I would call a customer. Lawyers turn customers into clients. Karen attended every important client meeting. An important client meeting is one where the lawyers are going to do the client in or overcharge him. In the legal trade this is known as sandbagging. Karen attended all of the meetings with George Nickleman. George Nickleman was often sandbagged.

George Nickleman was a very rich man. He was a confidant to the President of the United States of America and an alchemist of ideas. He turned the ideas into gold and banked the gold. Most of the profits from the Association of POW Wives and Families ended up in Switzerland in the Credit Suisse either that or in the hands of the Wall Street lawyers. He had everything a rich man could ask for. He bought each new offering of The Franklin Mint. Old Nickleman lived in Valdosta, had a beach house in Pensacola (a town in Florida) where he kept his yacht, owned an apartment in Chicago where he kept his mistress and leased a suite at The Drake to be near his fine lawyers. He shuttled between these four places in his very own Lear Jet.

The name Lear has nothing to do with the legendary king. It is the name of a man that makes jet planes for rich men. Nickleman's greatest pleasures were turning ideas into money without risking any capital and fucking.

"Maybe we could have a few drinks and a little supper later." Nickleman's thoughts shifted from torts to tarts once he and Miss Schuster were left alone.

"Well, I really have a lot of work to do." Miss Schuster wasn't taking any chances of offending the firm's best client. A best client is a customer that contributes the most money to a law firm year in and year out. Nickleman paid the firm vast sums of money. He owned a chain of grocery stores called Little Commanders. He started the Little Commanders to flog off the groceries collected by Dick Westcott during the Biafra famine. · The Little Commanders prospered and grew and Nickleman grew richer and richer. Nickleman hit upon the timeworn method of making lots of money: charging high prices, selling shabby goods and underpaying the help. He was able to do this by opening the Little Commanders early in the morning and keeping them open late at night and hiring one of the best law firms money can buy and knowing the President of the United States.

The Little Commanders, and there were about a thousand of them, were forever in some small trouble with the law: accepting food stamps for beer, paying less than the minimum wage, selling putrid meat, failing to comply with various Security and Exchange Control regulations, selling wine to minors and violating zoning codes. Miss Schuster's firm profited handsomely from this business by using junior associates and charging senior partner's rates. In most cases a mere change of date and place were all the work required on the legal papers. The senior partner said at every partner's meeting: "A few more like old Nickleman and we won't need any more probate work."

"Well that's all right. You can do all that tomorrow."

Nickleman was not the sort you would consider sexy. He was sixty, round of face and pudgy. With a gray wig and with a bun he could pass for a grandmother. The smell of dentures hung on his breath.

Still he was rich and had the power of the rich. If Henry Kissinger is sexy, then so too is George Nickleman. Karen felt a little stirring. Her inverted left nipple verted. The right nipple came to attention from the attention. She wasn't wearing her bra.

"I really have to..."

"Ah, come on." Mr. Nickleman was definitely looking cross-eyed. "You know, after dinner we can go to my suite and have a little fun, if you know what I mean." His left hand was on Miss Schuster's right knee.

Miss Schuster knew what he meant. Nickleman was not accustomed to being turned down. Karen must muster her fine education. Nickleman nurtured the quaint idea that girls that worked for the people he did business with had an obligation to hop willingly into bed with him. Not only that, he expected them to be extremely understanding and patient. Old Nickleman had good reason to believe his supposition. It generally worked with the giant food manufacturers, potato chip fabricators, real estate site selectors and advertising brokers. The fact of his hard prostate bothered him not one whit.

Karen Schuster had not spent the first eighteen years of her life on Long Island without learning a thing or two and said,

"Oh, Mr. Nickleman, I'd love to, but I can't, you see. I'm saving myself for my fiancée, he's a POW."

"My little dear, why didn't you tell me sooner. That puts a different light on it, yes indeedy it does. What did you say your young man's name was?"

"Justin Kleinschmidt. " It was the first time Miss Schuster had said the name or even thought of Justin Kleinschmidt in many a year.

"Justin Kleinschmidt"

"Ah, uh, yes." Miss Schuster thought she might have said the wrong thing.

Nickleman knew Kleinschmidt, she might have to fuck after all.

"That's my POW."

"Your POW?"

"Yes, yes, my POW, see." Nickleman took his left hand off Miss Schuster's left knee. He pulled back the green sleeve of his double knit jacket and there was a cupro-nic bracelet. The bracelet said: 2nd Lt. Justin Kleinschmidt, 0-96-34-382, October 28, 1967.

"Where on earth did you get that? I mean I didn't know that you knew Justin. " When Nickleman said that someone was his, he usually meant a bought judge or politician.

"You don't know about POW bracelets?"

"We used to have friendship bracelets in Great Neck. "

"Some POW's girlfriend you are."

"I've been working hard at the firm trying to forget the hardships that poor Justin must be going through. Its not easy, you know, knowing your fiancée is in that dreadful place."

"I can well understand and don't really blame you, little lady. He'll just have to get you one. Everybody wears one. Good Americans everywhere do. Even that Bolshevik Rubin Askew wears one. All Americans should. I'll get you one."

"That would be very kind."

"You see I am sponsoring life founder of the Association of POW Wives and Families." He thought he would get her a bracelet right that minute. Who knows he thought, maybe she will be grateful and they could still go to bed. His prostate felt the need of a massage.

"That's too much trouble, really."

"No trouble at all, little lady. I'm used to having my way." That is true. Nickleman used the firm's phone to call Dick Westcott in Los Angeles. Westcott told him about the meeting of the wives and families and Nickleman arranged for her to attend. He felt quite proud of himself. He felt the good American. Also he had hope for the future.

The entering of Miss Schuster's name confused the computer and caused the thing to have a bad memory. The machine got excited upon receiving Miss Schuster as the 586th attendee and pushed Mrs. Rex King out into the electronic void. The senior partner at her firm was a little confused when Nickleman told him Miss Schuster was going to California. But he knew Miss Schuster had many a lover in her time, and it was quite possible that one or more of them had ended up in one prison or another.

Soon Miss Schuster was on her way to the meeting of the Association of POW Wives and Families. Nickleman insisted she take the Lear Jet.

Richard Nixon made it to Key Biscayne without a hitch. He came on Air Force One, which is a jet plane and jet planes don't have hitches. It is a very comfortable way to travel. As soon as Mr. Nixon boarded Air Force One he took off his blue pinstripe suit jacket with the enameled American flag flying from the lapel. Then, as was his custom, he put on his Air Force blue nylon flight jacket. The jacket had the Presidential Seal embroidered in gold on the left breast. Under the seal were the words: Air Force One. Mr. Nixon Has very comfortable. He was not so comfortable once he reached Key Biscayne. Bebe Rebozo could not be found. Mr. Nixon had come all the way to Florida just to drink gin with Bebe Rebozo.

Bebe Rebozo thought he had the weekend off. He was dead wrong. Nixon would give him merry hell for not being there when he called. Poor Bebe had no idea that Mrs. King would cause Mr. Nixon to leave Washington in such a rush and come to Florida. Bebe planned on spending the weekend playing dominoes and drinking Cuban coffee. He preferred coffee to gin. Rebozo, by the way, means shawl in Spanish. Bebe, of course, is the common form of the Spanish verb beber--to drink. All over the Spanish-speaking world one sees signs saying: Bebe Coca Cola, Bebe Schweppes, Bebe Babycham, Bebe Tio Pepe. If there is a sign saying Bebe Rebozo, I've never seen it.

Bebe Rebozo stood his dominoes up on their long edge and smiled at the double sixes. He took a sip of the sweet dark coffee and rubbed his chest. He lit an Uppman cigar and watched the blue smoke rise. He smiled and said, "Thank heavens, I don't have to babysit the asshole this weekend." He said those words in Spanish. His partner smiled and said nothing--in Spanish or any other language.

Mr. Nixon was sitting in a comfortable lawn chair. He looked out at Biscayne Bay and brooded. Mr. Nixon broods a lot. General Haig came up to the man in the lawn chair and said,

"Milton Friedman is on the phone, Mr. President."

"Just who the fuck is Milton Friedman?" That is what the President said, honest.

"He is your economic advisor, Mr. President."

"Well, I am concerned about international affairs. I mean this President has more to do than concern himself with domestic problems." Mr. Nixon often spoke of himself in the third person. Any psychologist will tell you that that is a bad sign.

"He knows that and wants to talk to you about the worsening situation of the Italian Lira."

"Who gives a shit about the Lira? "

"I'll ask him that, Mr. President," said the General Haig. In case anyone is wondering, Milt Friedman is indeed an economist. He won the Nobel Prize in that subject. The Nobel Prize is often given to the wrong person. For all I know Milt Friedman might have actually deserved the Nobel Prize. It is a matter of speculation.

"Hey, General whatever your name is."

"Haig, Mr. President."

"Yes, it is Haig, isn't it? Hell, get me that Little Commander fellow. This President wants to talk about peace in our time."

"You mean George Nickleman, Mr. President. " General Alexander Haig has the mind of an IBM Systems III. Gen Haig was but a Lieutenant Colonel he served as aide to Henry Kissinger.

The one thing Dr. Kissinger can't stand is an aide smarter than he is. So Kissinger sold Haig to Mr. Nixon. Dr. Kissinger would make a superior IBM salesman. President Nixon made Haig a four star general. A four star general is just about the best sort of general there is. General Haig had never commanded a division, much less an army. He never would as long as Richard Nixon was around. Haig knew this full well.

"That's what I said, now get him on the honker now, don't argue." Mr. Nixon often called the telephone a honker.

"Right away, Mr. President." General Haig went off to call George Nickleman on the COSMIC DELTA line. Very secure, the COSMIC DELTA line.

Richard Nixon was deeply in George Nickleman's debt. Not money mind you, although it is rumored Mr. Nixon owes him a few hundred thou. Nickleman came up with the idea for the cloth coat, Checkers, China, George McGovern and of course, the POWs. Mr. Nixon was as grateful as he could be. Mr. Nixon has difficulty expressing gratitude. Thing was if anything went wrong with the POWs, or China for that matter, Mr. Nixon blamed George Nickleman. Nickleman thought if Pat lost a button off that respectable Republican cloth coat, Nixon would blame him. It was just awful when Checkers died.

"George Nickleman, the Little Commander guy on the COSMIC DELTA line, Mr. President."

"Nickleman, you old fuck, what do you mean trying to destroy the POW image. I mean this President won't stand for it. I'll have your ass."

"Dick, I don't know what you mean." George Nickleman didn't know what the President meant.

"You know, sending me that daffy dame for the photo opportunity."

"Daffy dame? You mean Karen Schuster? " Mr. Nixon did not.

"I can't remember. Maybe that was it."

"King, Mr. President. Her name was Regina."

"She's a little wacky, but she's very pretty, probably photographs very well."

"Pretty, photographs well, you gotta be kidding."

"I thought she was pretty. "

"You're a fucking pervert. Why that dame is fatter than any of Kalmbach's fat cats."

"She's got big tits, but I wouldn't call her fat, really."

"Her fucking tits are like watermelons."

"I bet she's something else in bed."

"Look Nickleman. Let's leave your own perverted ideas out of this. And I might say that I know a thing or two about perversion, not that I am an expert mind you, but I did serve in the Congress and under Eisenhower. So in the future forget your own kinky tastes and think images, the POWs and their impact on this President's second term."

"I'll do just that, Mr. President. "

Mr. Nixon hung up. "Haig or whatever your name is, bring me a large gin."

"Yes sir, Mr. President." Haig wished Manolo Rivera y El

Rey would hurry on down.

Sure enough when General Haig was off mixing a large Beefeater's gin--the President insisted on Beefeater's gin-- Manolo Rivera y El Rey showed up along with Lieutenant Roderick Vincent Wellborne III and the dispatch cases. Lieutenant Wellborne III wears the aiguillettes of a presidential aide. He calls it a fourragere, but then he went to Yale. Wellborne has the look of an aging choirboy. He looked like John Dean. If Richard Nixon had been Pope Urban VI he would have Wellborne fixed--fixed like Mrs. King's Siamese cat.

"I've brought the dispatch cases, Mr. President." General Haig showed up with the large Beefeater's gin. Haig, the keen observer, observed the gold cord on Wellborne's left shoulder and thought Nixon had commissioned John Dean into the Air Force.

Haig whispered in Nixon's left ear, "You can't have a lieutenant for an aide, Mr. President. It is wrong, that's for sure."

"Make him a captain. "

And that is what Haig did.

And so it was. Miss Karen Schuster attended the official meeting of the Association of POW Wives and Families. It was as strange as anything she had ever seen. And Miss Schuster had seen some strange things in her passage from Great Neck to the Wall Street law firm. Life had prepared her not. Her attendance was like walking into Bergdorf Goodman's and finding oneself in the souk at Marrakech.

It is not necessary to be a POW wife or family member to join the Association of POW Wives and Families. In fact only 0.0725% of the almost 5,000,000 members were wives and only 0.051216% were related in the remotest fashion to the poor POWs. They were merely basking in the reflected glory. The other 99.948668% were just plain good old-fashioned Americans, either that or CIA agents keeping an eye on things.

The meeting at the Century Palace Hotel in Los Angeles was expressly for the wives and families to prepare for the forthcoming homecoming. The meeting was to go on all day with a banquet that night. Rumor had it the President of the United States would appear. All the secret service men poking around lent substance to this wild and unfounded rumor. Until Mrs. King, the President had been looking forward to watching TV and drinking gin. The President always watched To Tell The Truth on Saturday nights. It was his favorite program. The President prided himself on catching the liars every time. Mr. Nixon is a man of some experience.

The POW wives met in the largest ballroom of the Los Angeles hotel. It w as called the Grand Ballroom. The room smelled of Joy perfume, and the clouds of smoke would make the Surgeon General weep. With few exceptions all the wives and family members were there. One exception was Mrs. King.

At the podium was the chairlady, Mrs. John H. Sloan, our hero's wife. Mrs. Sloan was a bit nervous. She spoke as a rule to small children, not to solemn convocations, but she had taken ten milligrams of Valium and seemed at ease. Valium is the trade name of the drug diazepam and is sometimes used as a substitute for gin, cigarettes and anti-perspiration preparations. She wore her new navy blue pants suit with a gold chain around the waist. Her nose was a bit too large for her face and her eyes deep-set. Her lipstick was a color that disappeared along with Betty Grable. Still in all she looked pretty for a middle aged lady. She was always elected president of this or that ever since she attended grammar school in Valdosta. She didn't like being a leader, but the role was always cast upon her. And now she chaired the Association of the POW Wives and Families.

Estelle Sloan married John H. Sloan reluctantly. She didn't aspire to great wealth, marrying, say, one of Valdosta's timber millionaires or a town doctor. She hoped for security and a nice house with a family room and a washer and dryer and a maid that came in three days a week and children that grew up to be cheerleaders and football players and a husband to take out the garbage. She had hoped for a husband that owned an appliance store or had a good job at the bank or was an accountant at Monarch Industries. She married instead John H. Sloan and had lived in a succession of rented apartments and houses. The Army life was not the life for the likes of Estelle Sloan.

She spoke. "I would like to welcome you all to a working meeting of the Association of the POW Wives and Families. Thank you all for coming. (Applause) Today we will go over Operation EGRESS RECAMP and the various methods of easing our men back into the 1970's. We have a senior Family Assistance Officer with us and a top civilian press officer from the Pentagon. I am sorry to say, or rather I am glad to say that Dr. Roger Shields, head of EGRESS RECAMP can't be here just now. Get this, ladies. Regina King is at this very minute meeting with the President of the United States of America. Dr. Roger Shields must wait by the phone in case the President needs him. Before I go on any more, I would like everyone to stand and give a big round of applause to Richard Milhous Nixon, the greatest President this nation has ever had because of what he is doing for our POWs."

The ladies stood and gave thundering applause. Miss Schuster had entered a world as strange as anything she had ever imagined.

"Before I introduce the first speaker, I'd like to remind everyone of you all to wear your POW bracelets. Oh, I know most of you all do, but I've heard (via Dick Westcott) that there are times, some occasions when some of us do not. He must show our support at all times even when we are in evening dresses. The Commies will never let our POWs come home if we don't support them. Also several new bumper stickers are now available, including--get this ladies--one saying: WELCOME HOME POWs."

Loud cheering and shouting interrupted Mrs. Sloan. Middle aged ladies jumped and shouted and clapped like high school cheerleaders after a touchdown.

"Thank you, thank you. I know you all are happy. Thank you. You all may obtain your stickers from National at the usual price (National's usual price included a huge markup). Dick Westcott is planning a nationwide newspaper campaign and that should sell a lot. Before I introduce Jerry Costheim of the Pentagon Press Office, are there any questions?"

No one ever asked questions at a meeting of the POW Wives and Families Association, so when Miss Karen Schuster arose, thousands of eyes were upon her. The eyes saw a pretty, well-cleaved young lady. The good will of the meeting died a quick death. She asked a question which was: "What about the paraplegics? Who is to welcome them home?"

"I don't understand." Mrs. Sloan didn't understand. A lot of the other ladies did.

"I mean you are planning a homecoming fort the POWs. Who's planning the homecoming for the wounded, the maimed, the blind, the paraplegics?"

The grossest indecency would have been better received. Even before Miss Schuster's indelicacy, she received more than her share of spiteful looks. She was casually, but expensively dressed, in fact, she was the only well dressed young lady in The Grand Ballroom. All but one of the other ladies wore pants suits. Some of them thought her a Communist agent.

Mrs. Sloan's eyes pleaded with Jerry Costheim for assistance. Costheim straightened his tie and stood. "It would be in poor taste for us to welcome home in a vulgar fashion, the paraplegics. The Government and the Veterans Administration are taking care of that."

"Thank you." Miss Schuster vowed to remain silent in this strange land.

"If there are no other questions, I would like Mr. Jerry Costheim to continue. Ladies, I give you Mr. Costheim." Mrs. Sloan gladly sat down. The diazepam wasn't quite doing its job.

Miss Schuster puffed a Winston Filter Tip cigarette. She decided to remain aloof, to take on the detachment of an anthropologist. At least she decided to try. Anthropologists make quite a show of detachment. She would make notes. Anthropologists are great note takers. Out came her Mont Blanc pen and her Mark Cross notebook. If you know any anthropologists owning a Mont Blanc pen and a Mark Cross notebook, I'd be pleased to know. Miss Schuster tried to reduce Costheim to writing. It couldn't be done. For Costheim, while sounding more than a little bit odd, was incomprehensible when placed on a page.

"The latest assessment of input makes for several viable options after allowing for random variables. Latest countermeasures with optimal regard to high technological devices render positive results on the bottom line. The data is (are?) responsive in this instance. " On and on, Costheim spoke on and on. The hysterical clapping lapsed into politeness. That didn't discourage Costheim and the words tumbled out. He might have been speaking beche-de-mer.

Karen Schuster and a lot of the other randy ladies noticed the zipper of Costheim's fly. It wasn't zipped to the top. Karen wore her contact lenses and could clearly see the little pull-tab sticking straight out--a miniature penis at half-staff. His trousers fit tightly and Karen wondered if he had been circumcised. You will never know.

Costheim graduated with an honors major in public speech from the University of California at Los Angeles (UCLA). He learned at that great center of scholarship that one must vary one's pace and timing in even the simplest of speeches. He was delivering a simple speech. Beware of coughing said the speech scholars at UCLA. A lot of coughing was going on in The Grand Ballroom. Whether this was the winter weather or filter cigarettes or smog or rudeness, I know not. Costheim did know that his professor told him to use a tried and true zinger, one always sure to get a round of applause as an antidote, as a cough suppressant. "Tried and true zinger" is an exact quote. Here is the zinger: "Remember that some of these guys (the POWs) don't even know who Lee Trevino is, so we must..."

The wave, the crash of applause should have won the professor of speech his tenure.

"So we must...Yes, Miss?"

"Who is Lee Trevino? " Miss Schuster really didn't know. Honest to God she didn't know.

Jerry Costheim, much the PR man, much the honor graduate of the University of California at Los Angeles, didn't miss a beat.

"We all know the strain you POW wives have been under and the whole nation is grateful for your suffering and understands." If there was any goodwill toward Miss Karen Schuster, an anthropologist wouldn't have noticed it.

Costheim talked on until his store of zingers emptied. "We will now break for coffee. There is coffee and I think the Association has provided Danishes at the rear of the room. After the break we will return to meet the Escort Officers. Meanwhile enjoy your coffee. Thank you, ladies. " Costheim wasn't going for any coffee. He was off for a quick gin in one of the many· bars at the Century Plaza Hotel.

To aid the reader with the chronology, I should point out that it was at this precise moment the guava bounced into the sandbagged engine house of the exercise yard in the Hanoi Hilton.

The wives and family members and the onetime girlfriend went for the coffee like addicts. Stupefied by Jerry Costheim, they would have gone for weak tea. None of the wives complained over Mr. Costheim's boring syntax and Miss Schuster didn't dare to. The wives chose to ignore the whole thing, rather than criticize the press officer (he was a civilian, but he was called a press officer nonetheless) from the five-sided building on the Potomac. Any hostilities vented themselves in the form of grumpy looks. The grumpy looks aimed themselves at Miss Schuster's tits.

There was coffee, instant coffee at the rear of The Grand Ballroom. Instant coffee is called instant coffee because it instantly looks like coffee when hot water is poured over a powder called instant coffee. It is a very successful product. There is also an instant tea. Instant tea cannot be explained.

There was no sugar at the rear of the room; only something called Sweet and Low. Sweet and Low is made with saccharine. Saccharine causes cancer of the bladder. Cigarettes cause cancer of the lung. Who would want cancer of the bladder? Who would want cancer of the lung? People, that's who. The good thing about saccharine and the good thing about cigarettes is they add not one single ounce to one's weight. Middle-aged ladies watch their weight.

There was no cream. Cream contains cholesterol. Cholesterol is essential to life itself. It is vaguely associated in most people's minds with blood lipids, fat in the blood. Who would want fat in the blood? Fat on the thighs and under the chin and on the belly is bad enough.

The Little Commanders provided something called a non-dairy creamer at cost plus a small handling charge. It was non-dairy. It was not a creamer. Remember a creamer? The breakfast table at grandmother's house had a creamer, a small slightly cracked pitcher filled with rich heavy cream from the top of the milk. In the summer when the grass was at its greenest and the cream at its heaviest, grandmother would spoon the cream from the creamer onto the children's oatmeal.

The label on the non-dairy creamer bragged: CONTAINS NO CHOLESTEROL. That is true. It didn't contain any eagle feathers either. It did contain: vegetable fat, coconut oil, corn syrup solids, sodium caseinate, di-potassium phosphate, mono-glycerides, sodiun1 silico aluminate, sodium tripolyphosphate, beta carotene, hydrolized plant protein, monosodium glutamate and artificial coloring.

By Danishes, Costheim meant Danish pastries. A Danish pastry is a splendid pastry made with yeast-raised dough. There were no Danish pastries at the rear of that room. There was something tasting of stale cardboard topped with pineapple flavored epoxy glue. The ersatz pastries were stale, elderly past the midnight standards of the Little Commanders. Old Nickleman graciously donated them from the stock of one of his day old bakery outlets. The Danishes were a good deal older than a day.

A day old bakery outlet is where the poor, the really poor, shop. The pastries freshly manufactured taste of fresh cardboard topped with pineapple flavored epoxy glue. Very few ladies finished their Danishes.

The Chairlady, Mrs. John H. Sloan, found herself standing next to Miss Schuster. Enough diazepam remained for her to calmly ask, "Is your husband a new shoot-down? "

Mrs. Sloan, we know, was an Army wife, but there were so many Air Force wives in the Association, she had begun thinking like them.

"I'm sorry, but I don't understand." Miss Schuster though down meant down, the downy feathers found on a duck's breast. The shoot must have something to do with hunting.

"Your husband, a new shoot-down?"

"Oh, I'm not married." Karen lit a new Winston filter cigarette from an old one and dropped the old butt into her paper cut full of instant coffee. The butt went Miss.

"Then why are you here? Why are you here making so much trouble?"

"Oh, my fiancee is a POW." That had got her out of trouble in the past. She wondered what kind of trouble she made. "He's a lawyer. I don't think he ever hunted. Sometimes lawyers take their good clients hunting so maybe."

"Oh." Mrs. Sloan wandered off looking for some place to leave her Danish.

An anthropologist might think a dress was the totem for the untouchables of the Association of the POW Wives and Families. Until Miss Schuster came along, Mrs. Lamar Butte, Sr. was the most disliked member of the Association. Mrs. Butte always wore a dress to the meetings. Mrs. Butte's dress was handmade--made with her own hands especially for this trip. She was a Mennonite and her dress reflected the code of that religion. She was an embarrassment to the ladies in the double knit pants suits. The dress was in terrible taste, even when judged by the standards of the Association of the POW Wives and Families. Like Miss Schuster, Mrs. Butte didn't wear a brassiere. Miss Schuster's right nipple showed clearly through the fine sea island cotton of her dress. Only the outline of the left Eisenhower silver dollar could be seen. Mrs. Butte's breasts hung like two empty hot water bottles. Her nipples pointed straight down and could not be seen through the heavy polyester blend. Mrs. Butte mothered a POW. Miss Schuster had at one time slept with a POW to be.

Both ladies were against the war. In Mrs. Butte's case, she was not only against the Vietnamese War, but all wars, all wars of any kind. Not only that, she was against the very military itself. Now our poor prisoners of war were professional military men and her alien belief sat very uncomfortably indeed on Association ladies. She was shunned. Being a Mennonite, she was used to a certain amount of ostracism and really didn't mind the snubs. Miss Schuster had yet to notice any ill will towards her. She thought the grim looks were looks of admiration.

Like nuns at Grand Central Station, like young wives at an office family meeting, like gynecologists at a Dow Chemical stockholders meeting, like insurance salesmen at the Rotary International, like misfits everywhere, Mrs. Butte and Miss Schuster found themselves together. Mrs. Butte said, "Howdy. "

That is what she said, so help me.

"Hi, " answered Miss Schuster. At least she said something like that.

"I don't know why I'm here."

"I know the cause, but not the reason. " Mr. Sterling didn't give all that money just to build a library and endow a few chairs at Yale. Mrs. Butte, anxious to talk, didn't know how to respond to Miss Schuster. Mrs. Butte knew little metaphysics.

"Is your husband a POW?" Miss Schuster is nothing if not understanding.

"No, my son, Little Lamar." Mrs. Butte's husband is known as Big Lamar.

"He's a prisoner?"

"I mean Lamar wasn't supposed to join; I mean we never brung him up that way."

"I beg your pardon." Maybe Mr. Sterling should have given a little more.

"It's the bounty, I'm sure the recruiters got a bounty. Why else would they want Little Lamar? I mean Lamar ain't too smart and they forced him into joining."

"You mean to say he was impressed?" Miss Schuster heard about that word in Great Neck.

"Maybe, he was an impressionable boy, that's what his teachers always said. How'd you know? I always said he was a nicen little boy, but I don't think he has sense to_ breed rabbits."

"And now he is a prisoner."

"So they say."

"And that is why you came?" Miss Schuster's mind still turned toward proximate causes.

"Well, you know, it was that Family Assistance man. He kept nagging me, nagging and nagging me. He said if I didn't come I would be letting the brave men down. That is what he called them, brave men. Why, I do not know. He said I would be letting the country, the President and God down. I never. As if I don't have enough to do, what with Big Lamar and the farm, without traipsin' all over the countryside."

"You mean to say you were impressed as well?"

"I ain't impressed with anything military."

The prisoners were lifers. That is not to say they were serving a life sentence. Mr. Le Duc Tho was trying mightily to get them checked out of the Hanoi Hilton. They were lifers in the service, in for twenty or thirty years. They were after their fat pensions. Thirty or even twenty years in the Army or even the Air Force seems a lifetime.

Major John H. Sloan was in for life, he hoped. Seventeen years in the Army and still a major is nothing to be proud of in today's Army. It might have been all right in the old days and even now it is all right in the British Army, but it is upwards or out now-a-days in the United States Army.

Major Sloan, that is what he called himself, looked every inch the old soldier. Years of living in the field, gallons of gin, and too much field kitchen food left him worn, hard and paunchy. He didn't believe in sunglasses and years of squinting gave him the eyes of an old fisherman. The wrinkles around his eyes put a crocodile to shame. The weather and the sun and the gin had done their work well. Seventeen years in the Army and six years in prison had left him a young old man at forty.

Sloan was a lifer. He wanted to soldier for thirty years; even then he wasn't sure that he wanted out. After all, what did he know besides soldiering and drinking gin? It is difficult to plan an Army career in prison. He thought about it a lot. Sometimes he would say out loud, "What the fuck am I doing here?" He wondered if the Army would count as good time his six years at the Hanoi Hilton, or would they discount it. Did the Army think he had put in twenty-three years or seventeen? Would the Army boot him out without a pension? What would he do?

What would he do for money? If his memory served him well and the scuttlebutt was true, all he would get for his six years in prison was $1.25 per day for missing rations. That was the rate for the survivors of the Bataan death march, a $1.25 a day. That is $2737.25 for six years away from garrison. Each day he added $1.25 to this total. What can you do with $2737.25? Buy a car, maybe. Have a damn good drunk in Saigon? If best came to best and the Army kept him, how would he stand as a major with twenty-three years service? Not well. If worst came to worst he'd spend some time in Leavenworth. Even if the Army didn't cast him in another prison, they'd drum him out of the service. He would have to buy a sword for them to break. His brass buttons would be cut off, his epaulets ripped off, his belt taken and he would stumble out of camp, no laces in his boots, to the tattoo of a single drummer. The reward for twenty-three years in the Army. He would face the world with boots flopping and pants drooping. Those were the rules. He had put up his hands and surrendered. A soldier is supposed to fight, not surrender. A more disciplined army would have him shot. If he didn't rot before his release, he would have to face the consequences of his own actions or hire a very good lawyer. Can one get a good lawyer for $2737.25? Would he even get that? "Forfeiture of all pay and allowances" stuck in his craw.

"Think positive, " said Justin Kleinschmidt.

"Think positive. Think positive for Christ sakes, Littlesmith. You sound like Norman Vincent Peale."

"Save us from that."

"I'd rather save us from Leavenworth. Surer than shit that's where we'll end up."

"That's not what the parachutists say. The new shoot-downs think they are some kind of heroes. I think some of them are pleased at being POWs."

"Fucking fly-boys are dippy."

"Maybe it's not as bad as you think. I mean you didn't sign an anti-war statement. A lot of the parachutists did and they still think of themselves as Colin Kelly"

"I didn't talk to Jane Fonda either. Besides, what kind of a soldier would sign an anti-war statement? Shit man, war's my trade."

"No war, no job, eh Jack."

"Just because we didn't sign an anti-war statement doesn't mean that they will let us off. Littlesmith, you're too young, but let me tell you about Colonel Frank H. Schwable."

"I know all about Schwable. We studied him at Camp Gordon." Justin Kleinschmidt had studied POH and International Law at the Judge Advocate Generals School at Fort Gordon, Georgia. It had made him somewhat of an expert on Southern drinking laws.

"Yeah, you're the fucking expert. So stop the Norman Vincent Peale shit about positive thinking. You know they will hang our asses. Some fucking lawyer you are."

"Look, I tell you again, the perfect defense. One, you must have not surrendered of your own free will. And number two, you must resist capture by all means available. That is the law. That is our defense. Nothing else counts. It is as simple as that."

"That's OK for the fly-boys, but we, you and I, fucking well surrendered."

That is true. And here is how it happened.

Sloan had a staff job, G-3 Operations at the Headquarters Troop of the First Cavalry Division. The horses of the First Cavalry Division had long been replaced by helicopters. Army veterans will remember the doggerel:

Hear the patter of little feet,

Here comes the First Cavalry in full retreat.

The First Cavalry was the first to leave the Yalu. General George Armstrong Custer commanded the Seventh Regiment of the First Cavalry at the Little Big Horn. The First Cavalry gathered what little glory it had there, not in Vietnam. A lot of brave men died in both places in the service of Garry Owen.

"Garryo, Garryo, Garry Owen. And you don't know where you're a-goin'."

Kleinschmidt, the Yale lawyer, a Judge Advocate General, attended the legal needs of the dead at the Headquarters Troop of the First Cavalry Division. The two men, Sloan and Kleinschmidt, so different in background, so different in education, so different in age became the friends men can only become in time of war. The war and the staff work drudgery drove them together. Sloan, the field soldier, hated staff work. He was too old to do anything else. Kleinschmidt, the Yale boy, hated the Army. He didn't know how to soldier. Kleinschmidt knew probate law the way a Wall Street lawyer knows corporate law. Kleinschmidt used to say and still might say for all that I know: "What kind of a fucking estate can a nineteen year old trooper leave? You do one you've done them all." A lot of nineteen-year-old boys died in the First Cavalry Division. It is an old tradition.

Kleinschmidt and Sloan took Sloan's jeep and drove into Danang looking for French food, gin and sexual congress. They found all three.

The French leave their mark wherever they go.

Their mark is good food. Up until the very last days of the war one could get a fine French meal in Danang or Saigon. The French are not much under mortar fire, but by God they can cook. Gin and whores are found wherever armies are found.

Sloan drove. Le Roy Kaiser was supposed to be Major Sloan's jeep driver, but Sloan drove. This made Le Roy Kaiser irate. He was, in his own words, "pissed off." And here is what he said at the time: "Fucking officers get all the mother-fucking breaks. I'm the fucking jeep driver. I should fucking well get laid just like the fucking officers. When my mother-fucking enlistment is up, I'm joining the mother-fucking Air Force." And so he did.

The two men drove up the old Highway Number One, across the Tourane River, past the Danang Air Force Base and into downtown Danang itself. In those days Danang was still a proper city.

The pink stucco bungalows of the civil servants and the old French colonial mansions with their wide verandas and the Jesuit churches and the palm trees and the wide lawns and the bougainvillea and the open markets and the squalid shacks made of Budweiser beer cans passed unnoticed by the men in search of food, booze and sex.

First stop was the old Colonial Hotel. Alas, it is gone now, but it was there then.

Kleinschmidt said, "Maybe we should rip off a little piece first."

"A man can't fuck without a little gin and a little food in his belly." Sloan was delaying. He wasn't sure he wanted to be untrue to Estelle.

"You don't know much about physiology, do you Major? But so be it."

On the east side of the Colonial there used to be a wide terrace with a view of the South China Sea. Flame trees with their cherry red blossoms hid what was left of the late afternoon sun. They sat down at one of the starched linen-covered tables. Each table was set for a full meal: two wine glasses at each place, crisp napkins folded in the shape of a fan nestled in the water glasses, a full set of cutlery--fish forks and knives, an army of spoons, and dinner forks larger than any Sloan had ever seen. The table had been set for four and two waiters carefully removed two of the settings.

"I'll have a gin and bitters, if you don't mind."

"Un kir, s'il vous plait."

"Oui, monsieur," said the captain, surprising himself. The menu was handwritten in French. There was a printed menu in English, but the captain thought to himself, if they want to speak French, they get the French menu. He thought that in Vietnamese, but I have translated for the sake of clarity.

"You order, Littlesmith. "

"Oui."

And here is what he ordered: an assortment of cold vegetables consisting of Celeri Remoulade, Garotte Rapee, Champignons au Citron and tomatoes with olive oil and sweet basil. The fish course was Quenelles de Brochette Nantua. And to please Sloan, Chateaubriand. Kleinschmidt told Sloan it was "steak pour deux." For wines, Boutard Montrachet and a fine bottle of Pommard. It was a splendid meal.

The whorehouses in Danang followed strict military protocol. There were whorehouses for enlisted men and whorehouses for officers. I am sad to say that the Colonial served as the whorehouse for the generals. The enlisted men thought that the officers got all of the really pretty girls. The officers thought the enlisted men got all the girls that knew the really fancy tricks. The generals did get the understanding girls.

The names of the whorehouses were something else— charming. The Purple Flower, The Passion Fruit, The Happy End, The Pink Horse, The Carrousel and Madame Fifi's. To Madame Fifi's went Lieutenant Kleinschmidt and Major Sloan.

It was an officer's whorehouse. The sign said: Madame Fifi's. Good Place. No VD. No Grunts.

"You go first Littlesmith, I think I'll have a gin first." Kleinschmidt went first. Kleinschmidt drank enough Montrachet and Pommard to try something that he had wanted to try ever since his days in New Haven. He could never bring himself to do it, but now was the time. The man and the whore had met. He mounted his whore, entered her and did nothing, nothing at all. He went in and didn't move at all. Now Danang whores are used to GIs that get it up, go in and get it off. It is a long time between fucks in Vietnam and it is over very quickly. Few Danang whores get sore. The whore smiled. No sweat, she thought.

But Kleinschmidt didn't cum. Hard as a rock he just laid there. The whore wiggled her ass and moaned and said, "You something, GI." Kleinschmidt remained hard in place. The whore, expecting the whole thing to be over soon slapped fast, a horse at full canter. Kleinschmidt stayed motionless. The whore said, "Come on, GI, you ding, ding." Kleinschmidt, hard as iron, did nothing. The whore went into a full gallop. She wished that she had used a little more K-Y jelly. She grabbed his testes. "You cum now, GI." Kleinschmidt didn't cum. The whore sweated, lathered, then rested. "You want suck suck, GI? No extra." Kleinschmidt didn't answer. He didn't move." You no fucking good, GI. You number ten. What's a matter you, you queer?" Kleinschmidt looked at the whore's tiny nipples, thought of Karen Schuster's silver dollars, pumped a few times and ejaculated.

"You something else," said the whore.

"Yeah, " said Kleinschmidt.

Sloan's turn came. He chose the same whore. The whore laced herself with K-Y jelly. The whore sucked Sloan hard. Sloan mounted, pumped three times and squirted. Sloan and Kleinschmidt were now brothers under the flesh. Sloan went downstairs and said to Kleinschmidt, "Let's have a gin and go back to base." They had another gin and left.

Sloan drove the jeep back down the Highway Number One and across the bridge spanning the Tourane River. There was a sign on that bridge that said: This bridge courtesy of The J89th Engineering Battalion (Airborne). The J89th Engineering Battalion (Airborne) had indeed put the bridge together, like one would put together an erector set. The bridge was named a Bailey bridge after Sir Donald Bailey. It was made by the Youngstown Bridge and Iron Company, Youngstown, Ohio. It was flown to Vietnam in 42 Lockheed C-141 jet planes. The Lockheed C-l4ls burned 4,636,832 gallons of J-2 jet fuel in their journey with the pieces of the bridge. This made the Texas oil men very happy.

Down the road a way they passed a sign saying:

Yes, though I walk through the Valley of the Shadow of Death,

I fear no evil,

Because we are the meanest Son-of-a-bitches in the valley.

THE FIRST MARINE DIVISION

Maybe, just maybe, the First Marines had nothing to fear. Sloan and Kleinschmidt also had no fear. They should have and would have if it hadn't been for all that gin and Montrachet. They didn't know it, but they were about to surrender to the Vietcong. For a young man Kleinschn1idt had a prostate that was just a little bit too large. Long fucking does the prostate little good. "Pull this vehicle over, Major, I've got to pee."

"Can't you wait?"

"Can a tidal wave wait?"

Major Sloan stopped the jeep and Kleinschmidt got out to pee. Sloan pulled out his Zippo lighter and lit a Winston filter tip cigarette. That was a mistake. Before Sloan could put his Zippo away and before Kleinschmidt could finish peeing, Russian AK-47 rifles were pointed at their heads. The Vietcong, twelve of them, dressed in black pajamas and B.F. Goodrich tennis shoes were holding those AK-47s. Lieutenant Kleinschmidt and Major Sloan were now POWs, prisoners of war. Kleinschmidt didn't even have a chance to shake.

And then there was the capture of Lieutenant Colonel Rex King. Here is how that happened:

Most prisoners became prisoners by jumping out of an airplane. They didn't jump actually, they ejected. Now-a-days Air Force jets simply go too fast for a pilot to climb out of the cockpit and onto the wing, jump off and pull the ripcord. An explosive charge rips the canopy off. A 40mm artillery shell explodes under the pilot's seat and hurls the pilot from the jet with the speed of a cannon ball. The parachute opens automatically by means of an aneroid barometer. The ejection of a pilot is quite a sight to see. It makes the death defying Ziembrowski of Ringling Brothers, Barnum and Bailey fame look the amateur. It is not much fun at the time for the pilot, but death defying it is.

The United States Air Force has countermeasures for all of the Russian rockets, including rockets the Russians haven't invented. The Russians spend a lot of time and rubles inventing rockets. Most all of the American planes were shot down by already invented Russian rockets. Air to air or ground to air rockets operate on a variety of principles according to their design and cost. The Russians, cheapskates as usual, supplied the North Vietnamese with old-fashioned rockets. The rockets were called for some reason or the other, SAM IIs, or more familiarly, SAM Also's. The SAM Also's homed in on the American planes by means of heat sensors, sound sensors, radar and old time ballistics. The latest Russian models use a combination of these methods as well as some techniques the CIA asked me not to mention. The surplus models supplied by the tightwad Russians to the NVA, the PRG and the VC were usually heat seeking and slow at changing their paths. Avoiding these SAM Also's is duck soup.

The United States Air Force trains its pilots well in the methods of avoiding the primitive Russian rockets. After all, the United States Air Force doesn't call its men the best-trained fighting men in the world on little authority. If the pilot does as he is trained, he would not and could not be shot down and will live to napalm another day. The usual method, the really surefire method taught by the Air Force is a little bit dangerous for the less than competent pilot and is uncomfortable in execution for those in bad physical condition. But it works.

The F-105 is a short winged plane and depends on its powerful, heat producing engines to stay aloft. The evasive technique called for the pilot to pull back hard on the stick as if to start a sharp climb and at the same time throttle back the engines. Do this and the aerodynamics of the F-105 fail.

It drops like Newton's apple. It would crash if it were a less powerful craft. It takes 15 seconds to avoid a SAM Also. By this time the earth is hurling upward at 350 miles per hour. In another few seconds the power of the General Electric engines would not be sufficient to restore flight and the F-105 would continue down until it met the earth. The pilot becomes a pat. After 16 or at most 17 seconds the pilot is supposed to apply full power and fire the afterburner. The plane with a terrible lurch overcomes the gravity and streaks skyward. The SAM Also can't recover and is wasted. The maneuver is hard on the pilot and the plane, but the pilot completes his mission and can return to base and drink a martini. There is little reason to be shot down over Vietnam by the bargain basement Russian SAM IIs.

Most pilots were captured because they were either lazy, ignorant, stupid, indecisive, inattentive, incapable, insolent, proud, presumptuous, optimistic, conceited, vain, drugged, drunk, tired, hungover or just plain scared. The maneuver could kill them if they didn't get it right. If the SAM Also's were after them and they pulled the ejection lever, the SAM Also would follow and destroy the plane with a great big bang whilst they floated gently to earth. In the waning days of the war, many men chose this method of life, especially after the POWs became the object of the hero cult.

Lieutenant Colonel Rex King pulled the ejection handle by mistake as the climb indicator spun downward. Bang out of the F-105 soared Lieutenant Colonel Rex King. There would have been more oooohs and ahs for Colonel King than there ever were for Mr. Ziembrowski, if somehow King could have ejected in Madison Square Garden. Talk about a human cannonball. Rex King was not drunk. He did not have a hangover. He was not a dope addict. He was a member of the Assembly of God and with that a lay preacher. Booze and dope never entered his body. He admonished the younger on their sinful ways. He wanted them to give themselves to Christ. Giving oneself to Christ means giving up booze and dope. It is not a popular idea.

Age and neurosis caught up with Colonel King and the good doctors of the Air Force prescribed a variety of amphetamines and tranquilizers. King, not schooled in pharmacology, took the pills in the wrong combination and pulled the ejection lever instead of the throttle as he passed over the 17th parallel. He was surprised at being a human cannonball. He said, as he shot from the cockpit, "Jesus fucking Christ. "

Lieutenant Colonel Rex King floated to earth only to be met by Pohn Van Ngo, Sr. Pohn Van Ngo, Sr. spent all of his spare time looking for American pilots. He was there waiting in the rice paddy for King to land. He calculated the wind drift. His son, Pohn Junior, was studying English at the Hanoi Institute of Technology (HIT) and he met all the American pilots he could. He always asked for any English books they might have. His first words to Lieutenant Colonel King were, "My son is studying your language at the Hanoi Institute of Technology. I would be pleased if you would be so kind as to give or rather lend me any books in English you might have. It would greatly help my son's education. He is studying your English." Pohn Van Ngo, Sr. spoke those words in Vietnamese. King didn't understand one word. He put up his hands. Pohn Van Ngo, Sr. smiled and said, "Any English books. Ones you have read, of course. " He spoke the only language he knew. King gave him his scarf saying in five languages (English, French, Spanish, Chinese and Russian), "I am an American pilot." Pohn Van Ngo, Sr. said, "Thank you very much. What a nice scarf. Mrs. Pohn Van Ngo, Sr. will surely like to have it. You have some English books maybe?"

Rex King spoke only English. Pohn Van Ngo, Sr. spoke only Vietnamese. This made communication difficult. Pohn started a pantomime of a man reading a book. He hoped the man looked like an Englishman. He didn't. King handed him his Colt 45. Colt 45 is the name of a pistol made by Colt Industries in Hartford, Connecticut. It is made for the express purpose of killing human beings. Pohn Van Ngo, Sr. thanked him in Vietnamese and continued his pantomime. King gave him his Air Force identification card, his codebook, his kneeboard with the TOP SECRET cruise control card and radio frequencies. Pohn was thanking him, when three aged members of the Peoples Provisional Home Guard (PPHG) doddered up. The PPHG was suggested by Mr. Le Duc Tho to enable double amputees and golden agers to have a feeling of pride of serving their country in time of war against capitalist hordes. The PPHG took King off to the Hanoi Hilton. Pohn Van Ngo, Sr. was later made a Hero of the Peoples Republic of Vietnam. The cruise control card, the codebook and especially the radio frequencies helped the war effort mightily.

Private Lamar Butte, Jr. slept his way into prison. One thousand one hundred and eighty-eights, also known as eleven eighty-eights, sleep a lot. Private Lamar Butte, Jr. was a small man. Army policy calls for small men to be turned into jeep drivers, cooks or company clerks. The instrument of Army policy is an IBM 360/65 in the basement of the five-sided building on the

Potomac. Not many people know how to program an IBM 360/65 properly, least of all Army people. The Army made a goodly number of small men into radio operators. In the Army a radio operator is the person who carries the darn thing. Little Lamar carried the PRC-39, the radio the Army uses when it wants to talk with the Air Force. Private Lamar Butte, Jr. has a slight humpback as the result of tuberculosis of the spine when he was but a small bit of a lad. This made the carrying of the PRC-39 at best awkward and at worst painful. It was a shameful thing for the IBM computer to do.

Lamar used to say, "This (the radio) is a heavy son-of-a-bitch." He took it off every chance he got. As the radio operator, Little Lamar had to go on every patrol his company took. He had to carry the heavy radio. One dark night in 1968 the patrol took a break shortly after midnight. Lamar took the PRC-39 from his back, lay down and went to sleep. When the platoon moved on, they didn't remember Little Lamar. They hardly ever remembered Little Lamar unless they wanted to talk to the Air Force. He was still asleep when the Vietcong found him around ten the next morning. And that is how Private Lamar Butte, Jr. became a prisoner of war. The Vietcong were pleased beyond measure to get the PRC-39. It gave them a slight edge on the United States Air Force, now that they had Colonel King's codebook and frequencies. They looked at Little Lamar and shook their heads. One senior officer said, "Americans must be scraping the bottom of the barrel. War be over soon." Scraping the bottom of the barrel is a common cliché used by the Vietnamese.

It was time for the meeting at the Century Place Hotel to resume. Danishes stood on and under the tables. Some Danishes sat on the ballroom chairs. None were finished. The room was littered with unfinished Danishes and paper cups half full of instant coffee and cigarette butts. The butts floated in the instant coffee. The ashtrays were overflowing with Danishes, cigarettes butts, paper napkins and used Kleenexes.

The place was a grand mess and the real business of the Association of POW Wives and Families had yet to start. The blowers were going full tilt. They didn't stand a chance. They couldn't keep pace with the cigarette smoke no matter how much racket they made. The Grand Ballroom smelt of cigarette smoke, stale cigarettes, stale epoxy glue, gin, Joy and Los Angeles smog. The air conditioning system bled 18% fresh air in strict accordance with the architect's specifications. The fresh air smelt of smog. Smog is the name for bad smelling air. Yellow and green air are also called smog. Blue air is called sky. Gray or white air is called clouds, unless the gray or white air is close to the ground. Close to the ground if the air is truly white or gray it is called fog, otherwise it too is called smog. Black air is generally called night.

A small Honeywell computer automatically reduced the speed of the blowers whenever someone used the PA system. Honeywell is the name of the company that makes computers that do such things. A PA system is a device for making someone sound louder than they really sound. If the blowers weren't told to hush, no one could hear a thing--PA system or no PA system.

The real business was about to start. The ballroom was full. It was full with wives and family members and military men of all sizes and shapes. Some of the military men were the Escort Officers and they were there as a special treat for the ladies. The Escort Officers were going to meet the POWs when they got on the plane in Hanoi and stay with their men, attending to their every need and whim. There was one Escort Officer for each and every one of the prisoners. Few enlisted men were prisoners so there were enlisted Escort Officers. While they were enlisted men, they were called Escort Officers. Such is the logic of the Pentagon.

All of the Escort Officers were selected because they were Xerox copies of the poor prisoners. They were of the same rank, had the same family size, the same hobbies, the same education, the same vices, the same eyes, the same thoughts and the same military specialty as their counterparts at the Hanoi Hilton. They could swap shoes. An IBM 360/65 did this. The numbers 360/65 have something to do with how much the thing costs. The machine, which costs a good deal of money, coughed up 586 more or less identical copies right down to sock size. Some of the wives found this disquieting. One wife, a nice lady from California, said, "Shit, I should have voted for McGovern. "

The IBM 360/65 using a programming system known in that trade as OS/VS2 produced not only a Lamar Butte, but a Lamar Butte judged competent to go to Hanoi and keep his man out of the rain. That was not an easy task and is a testimony to the IBM 360/65's computing skill and fine memory. The IBM 360/65 only forgot things when it was confused or let its mind wander. The thing found a Justin Kleinschmidt right down to his membership in Morys. That was kid's stuff for this fine computer. The machine balked a bit on John H. Sloan. The IBM 360/65 made whatever noises a hard thinking computer makes. It whirred and clanked and then coughed up a John H. Sloan more or less. I am sure the machine did the best it could. The easiest trick of all was finding a Rex King right down to his hobby of Turtle waxing his Thunderbird. A Thunderbird is an automobile, so help me. By the time the Escort Officers met the prisoners of war they would be ex-prisoners of war, but they would be known as POWs for the next five or six years. After that they would be known as people.

The Escort Officers weren't the only military men in the Grand Ballroom. The wives had had something called a Family Assistance Officer for some years. Now there wasn't one for each and every wife, budget cuts had seen to that. There was one for every two wives or in the few cases of enlisted men or junior officers, one for every three. The Family Assistance Officers provide, in the words of Department of Defense Order Number DOD 16432-85.6 Rev 2.3: "All due assistance to the next of kin of all military personnel incarcerated or now held by the Peoples Republic of Vietnam (North Vietnam)." The order further defines next of kin. Military personnel were defined as members of the Armed Forces of the United States of America, Central Intelligence Agency (CIA) agents or employees, civilian contractors to the United States Government and deserters not found guilty of desertion at a General Court-martial.

The assistance was defined, but not limited to the finding of base housing, assistance in obtaining military pay and allotments and PX privileges and in keeping the families informed in a general way of the status of the prisoners.

The job of a Family Assistance Officer (FAO) is not all that easy as any FAO will tell you. They had to speak at public meetings, called appropriate forums. The appropriate forums were such things as PTA meetings, church groups, Rotary Clubs, Lions Clubs and the like. Even if there were any lions in a Lions Club it would still be a boring job.

The Family Assistance Detachment was a huge group, what with the three levels of supervision, the liaison officers with the Congress, the major branches of government, the White House, the CIA and various embassies. There was a Public Information Sub Section (PISS) that sent out press releases to the wire services and the POW's local newspaper. The Motion Picture Sub Section (MPSS) furnished film clips to the television networks. All in all the FAO Detachment had 3,087 men. In fact the TO&E (Table of Organization and Equipment) called for 3,183. A listing of equipment would be boring.

The Commanding Officer of the FAOs was a Navy Rear Admiral. A rear admiral is the most junior of admirals. General Haig wanted an Army man for this most important post and made his feelings known at the highest level of Government. Admiral St. Thomas More always bad a real feeling for things at the White House and of course found out about Haig's doings. He said at the time, "I headed the bastard off at the pass. "

The Honeywell computer told the blowers to shut up. The Assistant Deputy Commander (Operations) spoke: "I am sure your FAO has briefed you all on the REPAK file. Remember the REPAK file will be the first printed word from the good old U.S. of A. It will be the first word your man has from you. I will go over the parts of the REPAK one more time for the sake of clarity. Briefly that is (loud applause). Thank you (he smiles). Thank you very much. Well briefly the REPAK has three parts, just like Gaul (he laughs). Hell, part one is called the brochure and it is a complete file of pay, promotions and military savings accumulated since shoot-down. I guess that most of the boys know that already. (He laughs again.)

"Part two is called the private file. Here's where we need your help. That is the reason for today's meeting. Immediately after this session your FAO and EOD Officers will meet privately with you and give you any help you might need on your letter. You will help him by providing any missing information needed to complete the private file. Briefly the private file will have family info on marriages, divorces, deaths, births and so forth. It will have your letter. Remember that these men have been out of touch for a long time, some for a very long time. We would also like some personal item, say a pair of slippers or a favorite pipe; well you know what I mean. Have no fear about anyone else reading your letter. Your FAO will provide at no cost to you the paper and pen and of course the envelope. He will help you with your spelling and give you a few ideas on what to say. For heavens sake don't say anything to upset your man. Be upbeat. As I say, the letters will be sealed by yourself, so all of us, President Nixon included, are placing our trust in you."

Each and every letter was steamed open. Most were lovely touching letters, letters only long separated lovers could possibly write. The ladies poured the thoughts and yearnings of the long lonely years onto those pages. Some were faintly erotic and a few frankly pornographic, but all were lovely. The censors were looking for things that might upset the unbalanced, and since that was their job, that is what they found. Some of the tender words, in fairness to the censors, possibly could upset those of delicate sensibilities. The CIA provided forgers to copy over all of the letters, leaving out the marked passages; thereby changing the meaning, the mood of those impassioned, rapturous letters forever. It is said that the forgeries were technically perfect.

"Part three is called the history file. This will bring your man up to date on all the things that have happened since he's been a prisoner. It will contain past Super Bowl scores, for example. We used the Readers Digest staff. He had them tailor each man's history file to his interests and shoot-down date. If he likes golf, we tell him about Lee Trevino." The Assistant Deputy Commander (Operations) stopped speaking and waited for the applause.

The applause didn't come. There was silence all around. The zinger was not negotiable. The silence fooled the Honeywell computer. It thought the speech was over and turned the PA system off and the blowers on. Now turning the blowers on and waiting around for someone to use the PA system is a very boring job even for a Honeywell computer. The Honeywell let its mind wander. It started thinking about the IBM Systems III in the accounting office. When the Deputy Commander tried to talk, he couldn't be heard. The Honeywell computer forgot all about the PA system. It was consumed with lust and making lewd noises. The blower's roar hid the computer's sound and the Deputy Commander's voice. The blowers did a good imitation of the Concorde landing at Dulles International Airport.

The American fighting man's ingenuity is the source of great pride for the admirals and generals. All the FAOs and EODs had graduated from a school called the Ingenuity Training and Command School (ITCS). It was not a waste of their time or the taxpayers' money. The FAOs and the EOD Officers used some of the ingenuity learned at ITCS and went on to the next item on the agenda without being told. They sought out the families they were supposed to assist. The officers remembered their dictionaries, the pink paper and envelopes and ballpoint pens. The ballpoint pens were embossed in white:

OPERATION EGRESS/RECAMP DOD 67031274 Mark IX (all others obsolete).

"Miss Schuster, I'm Major Barry Block," shouted Major Barry Block. "And this is Captain Tom Gilliam, Captain Kleinschmidt's EOD Officer." The Major's left eye pointed at Miss Schuster's right nipple and his right eye pointed to where her left nipple should be. He had the look of one of Mr. Disney's myopic automatons.

Miss Schuster brought her left hand up to scratch her right collar bone, effectively hiding the shape of her bosom and the imprint of her right nipple. "How nice," yelled the young woman as she walked away.

"We are here to help you with your letter." Major Block was a college graduate. His eyes were no longer crossed. Captain Gilliam was, of course, a Yalie. His eyes were still crossed.

"Please, I don't need your help. I got to get the fuck out of this mad house." She had long ago put her Mont Blanc pen and her Mark Cross notebook back into her Gucci bag. The bag is called a Gucci bag because it bad the word GUCCI printed on it in large white letters.

Military men call a woman that doesn't wear a bra fair game. Not all women; not Mrs. Lamar Butte, Sr. for example, but most women. Miss Schuster was classified as fair game. The FAOs, it had long been rumored, were used to taking certain liberties, shall we say. When Karen said fuck the two officers's eyes lit like sparklers.

"How about a drink?" screamed Captain Tom Gilliam in his loudest voice.

"Sounds good." Anything to get out, thought Miss Schuster. The three left the large hall, the noisy ballroom. The two officers jockeyed for position along side the fair game. Their lust was as formalized as the mating ritual of the Ugandan Nob. The two officers in their military finery, chests swollen, eyes bright and slightly crossed, pulses rapid, penises rising caused considerable envy amongst their peers, their fellow FAOs and EOD Officers.

Miss Schuster and the two bucks made it to the nearest bar, which was called Nell Gwynne. The din could still be heard in the distance. The bar was California's impression of how a 17th Century English pub might have looked if plastic had been around in the 17th Century. Each of the many bars had what the hotel called a different motif. Each motif tried for a different century. The motifs weren't all that authentic and so the management provided little signs that told the century.

The barmaids were called serving wenches and the drinks were called grogs. There was a small buffet set up on what was called a groaning board. All of the help and some of the customers appeared to be in drag.

The two officers foolishly ordered martinis. Miss Schuster ordered a kir. Miss Schuster first had to spell kir for the serving wench. That didn't work, so she wrote it out on one of Major Block's pink pieces of stationery.

On each table in the Nell Gwynne rested a red votive candle. The red glass bulb covered with monofilament fishnet smelled of Bayonne, New Jersey. The manufacturer, a large oil company, advertised and warranted these candles as an effective mask for cigarette smoke. That is true. The Nell Gwynne smelled like Bayonne might smell if cigarettes were banned in that lovely town. The oil company called the votive candles BAR FLYS. The candle wax, if it can properly be called a wax, was the by- product of the refining process. The refiners among themselves called the wax a low petroleum distillate or more familiarly LPDs. LPDs are a source of annoyance to oil men. They clog the condensers and filters. They smell. They burn unevenly. They sometimes explode. They don't float. They can't be dumped in a river without sooner or later causing a flood. In times gone by, the refiners buried the LPDs or barged them out to sea. Ask any oil refiner what he thinks of low petroleum distillates and he will always answer, "LPDs are a pain in the ass."

Do-gooders often pestered the oil companies about LPDs. The oil companies, quick to respond to the public interest, hired a moonlighting scholar from The B School. Until that moment the man had specialized in the packing of meat. In a couple of days at 82.50 the day, the scholar came up with the BAR FLYS.

The product is also sold under the trade name of BUG OUT. The only difference is the color of the glass. It is yellow. The scholar couldn't imagine that insects might actually like the smell of Bayonne. BUG OUTs are very popular items and can be found on patios all over America.

Miss Schuster didn't know it, but her law firm was responsible for the monofilament fishnet. The netting satisfied the Consumer Protection Act of 1969. In other words, if the BAR FLY or BUG OUT exploded, the maimed and blinded would have no recourse under law. Karen's firm was the best in the business. They never sandbagged an oil company.

Little announcement cards cluttered the table. One called the piano player a minstrel. Another thought that Nell Gwynne put out for Henry VIII. The management, confused about a lot of things, confused Henry VIII with Charles II. It is a small point.

A little bowl filled with little pink bags of saccharine nestled close to the BAR FLY. The saccharine was thoughtfully put there by the management to sweeten their famous Irish Coffee. Their Irish Coffee was made from non-dairy creamer foam, instant coffee, saccharine and cheap Kentucky whiskey. It was a very popular item. People were known to come from as far away as San Clemente just to drink an Irish Coffee at the Nell Gwynne.

"This is really a great place. Just look at those beams. I wonder where they found them? " They found them in a chemical factory, Major Block. The beams were made of polystyrene phenylethylene.

"Outstanding," said Captain Tom Gilliam.

Miss Schuster felt vaguely ill, slightly sick in the stomach, but she tried at conversation. She was not unmindful of the two officers' lust and found it in a way agreeable. "How do you like being a family whatever you are, Major? "

"Family Assistance Officer, it's a piece of cake. "

"Are you a supply or commissary or whatever it is as well? "

"Me, I'm the Escort Officer for Captain Kleinschmidt," answered Captain Tom Gilliam out of turn.

"You mean Lieutenant Kleinschmidt?"

"No, Karen, I can call you Karen, can't I? Captain Kleinschmidt, it says so right here."

"Then you've got the wrong girl, excuse me please."

Miss Schuster stood.

"No, no, please sit down. You've got a drink coming. Your man received two promotions so far. Look, Justin Kleinschmidt promoted to First Lieutenant on January 21, 1969 and to Captain on 17 June 1972."

"How on earth could they promote someone twice while he is in a prisoner of war camp? How could they promote someone who surrendered to the enemy or at least to the North Vietnamese? They wouldn't do that surely. They couldn't."

The two officers looked at each other with eyebrows raised. Their lust dimmed a bit. Major block was about to defend the promotion system, when the serving wench turned up with the martinis.

"The keeper of the royal grog sends his regrets, but he has no cur, me lady."

"No, shit." Miss Schuster learned that response at Barnard. The serving wench unmoved asked, "May we bring you something else, me lady?"

"A beer, any kind of a beer but a Budweiser or a Coors."

"I like Bud," said Major Barry Block.

"I like Coors," said Captain Tom Gilliam.

"That is all we have, me lady," said the serving wench.

"Bring me a Coke," said Miss Schuster.

"Ah..." Major Block could think of nothing to say. The two military men had little in common with the lady lawyer. Major Barry Block decided to play his ace. "I am to personally deliver this Christmas card from Richard Milhous Nixon, who sends his warm regards and felicitations."

The card said:

Seasons Greetings and

Peace on earth from the

President

Of

The United States of America

(signed) Richard M. Nixon.

Miss Schuster read the card and handed it back. "No, no it's for you."

"I don't want the fucking thing."

"Why not?" Major Barry Block was genuinely shocked.

"He's got a lot of goddamn nerve, that's why."

"What do you mean?" Even Captain Tom Gilliam was puzzled and Captain Gilliam went to Yale. Yale is supposed to unpuzzle people.

"The cocksucker is bombing the shit out of Hanoi and he wants to wish me peace on earth?"

"That's no way to talk about the Commander-in-Chief. Suppose some Commie heard you. You should be ashamed. You are a POW wife." Major Block was wrong about Karen being a POW wife. We know she wasn't. There were no Commies in the Nell Gwynne as far as I know. To be sure the AFOPs ordered quite a lot of bombing, but I doubt they were really bombing the shit out of Hanoi. Power plants, yes; Le Duc Tho's villa, yes; people, yes; hospitals, yes; train stations, yes; flower markets, yes; cafes, yes; water works, yes; shit, no. There is no recorded evidence whatsoever that President Nixon engages in fellatio. It was a cruel thing for Miss Schuster to say. The President might have indeed wanted to wish Miss Schuster peace on earth. Nixon thinks of himself as a peacemaker.

"She's been under quite a strain." That phrase comes up often in the POW business. Captain Gilliam still lusted after Miss Schuster.

"The only strain is you two dopes. Tell the President to stick the Christmas card up his ass. No don't tell him that, it sounds like something he might enjoy." That was a malicious thing for Miss Schuster to say. I don't think she really thought the President would like to have the card so inserted. But that is what she said and it caused the now Captain Kleinschmidt's REPAK file to only have two of its three parts.

It was high season at the Hanoi Hilton that Christmas of 1972. When the bombing stepped up, so did the new arrivals. Each day five or six American pilots checked in. During Christmas week alone forty-three parachutists joined the other sad guests, putting a strain on the small staff of the Hanoi Hilton. Each new man expected brutal treatment. The Pentagon indoctrinated their men to such a degree the men were, in their own words: "scared shitless." Each man, before being allowed to bomb Vietnam, viewed twenty hours of films telling him what to expect if they happened to eject. I've seen films of the birth of a calf that weren't nearly so gruesome. Some men had even been through a mock prison camp in North Florida near Fort Walton. The training program's climax came with the showing of a film clip of Richard Milhous Nixon made on April 17th, 1971. The leader of the Free world said, "The North Vietnamese without question have been the most barbaric in [the] handling of prisoners of war of any nation in history. " The new guests found little comfort in Mr. Nixon's words.

Sometimes the staff of the Hanoi Hilton was more than rude. It depended on the individual guards. The guards, being people, were mean and kind, generous and stingy, curious and apathetic, skeptical and trustful, guileless and bitter, truthful and mendacious, smart and stupid, idle and enterprising, cowards and heroes and good and bad. Some shared their dark Vietnamese tobacco with their charges. Sloan called these guards R. J. Reynolds. The dark tobacco was strong and smelled, stank of burning garbage. It is necessary to smoke it in small puffs. Other guards took what tobacco the prisoners had. He called these guards Surgeon Generals.

Kleinschmidt spoke the sort of French taught in New Haven. All the guards over forty spoke French of the sort taught by the French when they were in charge of Vietnam. The French called Vietnam Indochina. Kleinschmidt, the expert in POW law and in French, often acted as advocate for the other prisoners. Other times, he just chatted with the guards. One of the guards, a chap named Nguyen Thanh Linh liked to brag, "You Americans just think you are smart, but Vietnamese smarter."

Kleinschmidt always answered, "How come you're not winning the war then?"

"If we're not winning, how come you're a prisoner?"

"Bad luck."

"Bullshit." Now Nguyen Thanh Linh didn't really say bullshit, but that is what he meant. It is not a bad translation.

"Look at all the stuff we have. " An exact translation.

"Yes, Americans have plenty stuff. You Americans even tried to use dogs to sniff out Vietcong. But we fool dogs. We fool Americans. Vietnamese smarter."

"I don't understand. "

"We fool dogs. Use Dial soap. That way dogs no can find. Dumb American dogs think that Vietcong are GIs."

"Dial soap? Where on earth did the Vietcong get Dial soap?"

"Buy at your PX. Sometimes we bought Lifebuoy."

"At the PX?"

"Sure, at the PX. Americans are capitalist. Capitalists like to sell things. We bought all kinds of supplies at PX. Most of the stuff no fucking good. We could buy anything except Winston cigarettes and Johnnie Walker.

The prisoners thought and talked a lot about their wives. Rex King, for example, thought about Mrs. Rex King. Regina King lost ten pounds a year in Lieutenant Colonel King's mind. As the years rolled by, off rolled the pounds. In real life Regina King gained ten pounds a year. If Le Duc Tho has his way, Rex King will soon be in for a big surprise.

Little Lamar had never had a girlfriend, much less a wife. If he thought of a woman, that woman was his mother. His thoughts were mainly the way she cooked. Mrs. Lamar Butte, Sr. was a wonderful cook. From time to time Little Lamar had an erection. Lamar felt nice when his penis reached for the sky. He also felt guilty. Mrs. Lamar Butte, Sr. always said when she caught him playing with himself, "Lamar, don't do that. It will make you crazy." The last thing Little Lamar wanted to be was crazy. Crazy people are not held in high regard in Valdosta, Georgia.

Kleinschmidt's loves were a blur of pretty women. In the ten years before prison he had had at least fifty pretty women. Five a year, sometimes more. Miss Schuster could barely be made out in the rush. All Kleinschmidt could remember was a parade of pretty women reaching back, unhooking their bras and pulling down their panties in one graceful swoop. One was pretty much like the other. Some liked the lights off, some didn't.

John H. Sloan didn't talk much about Mrs. Sloan. He though about her a good deal of the time, but he didn't talk about her. He knew that she didn't want to marry him and had given in more than saying yes. Sloan conducted a courtship worthy of a drawn- out military campaign. The siege lasted three years, the ramparts crumpled slowly. Estelle's father opposed the marriage. At some sacrifice, the father had paid her way through the University of Georgia. Sloan only graduated from Valdosta's high school. A diploma from Valdosta High is worth about as much as a last years World Series ticket. Sloan was known to drink. He was not a drunk, far from it, but he drank. Estelle's family was Baptist. Sloan's family never amounted to a damn and as the father said, "Neither will he. He's nothing but a soldier, a common soldier."

"Why Sloan courted with such zeal is something he couldn't remember. Maybe it was the way she smiled or the tilt of her head when she laughed or the gentle way she touched his penis when they petted. Or perhaps it was her basic shyness. You would have to know her well to know the depth of her shyness. Maybe it was the way she held out for so long that kept Sloan's interest. Maybe it was some primal imperative, some need of the species demanding the mating. Sloan persisted and Estelle gave in when her high school sweetheart, Bill Cobb, married the daughter of one of the timber millionaires.

The marriage lasted. It was not what you and I would call a happy marriage, but it lasted. Two animals in the same cage, two travelers sharing the same cabin on a long ocean voyage, they somehow got along. Estelle didn't really care for lovemaking. In the last few years of the marriage, she only gave in when Sloan became too restless or returned from duty in the field.

They fucked, that is what it was, maybe once a month. They didn't sleep together before they were married. Estelle was a virgin. They did lie together naked a few times and kissed for hours. Once, almost a year before the marriage, Estelle masturbated him. She ran from the room when the semen came. It was three days before she would even talk with him over the telephone.

During the first few weeks of their marriage they made love two, sometimes three times a day. It was a new experience for the new Mrs. Sloan and she was determined to find out what all the fuss was about. Then Estelle developed cystitis and the honeymoon was over. The urologist called it honeymoon bladder as he smiled and rubbed her clitoris ever so slightly. Then he charged her $10.00 for the visit. That was a lot of money in 1957.

Sloan worried how his wife must feel with him in prison. It just had to be hard on her. He could hear her father's words mocking her and him. He felt guilty about the Danang whore.

He seldom had a whore and never had a girlfriend once he married. He didn't think a man his age should masturbate and only visited a whore when the semen cried for release. He always felt guilty and brought his wife little presents when he returned. The disgrace of the Court-martial and the possibility of Leavenworth would surely end the marriage. It was very sad. Sloan worried about Leavenworth and the Court-martial and their effect on Mrs. Sloan. What a way to end an Army career, no wife, no pay and in Leavenworth. It didn't seem fair. Still, he had surrendered and that is the way things would be.

Sloan only shaved every fourth or fifth day and he had the look of a Bowery bum in his faded black prison suit. The senior ranking officers tried to enforce a measure of military discipline and threatened Sloan with a bad fitness report if he didn't shave daily. The senior ranking officers only understood how to argue amongst themselves about who was really the senior ranking officer. They bore no compassion for Sloan. Sloan ignored the senior parachutist's threats. After all, what's a bad fitness report compared to a Court-martial? Who would read his fitness report after he was drummed out of the Army?

"Tell me some more about our rights, Littlesmith." Sloan was trying to cheer himself.

Kleinschmidt looked at Sloan's stubble and quoted Article 55.5 of the 1923 Geneva Accord verbatim, "Prisoners of war shall be allowed at all times to obtain hot water at reasonable prices, not to exceed five centimes or five pfennigs for two liters."

"What's a centime or whatever it is?" Little Lamar was a curious lad.

"That's French money, son." Sloan had served in France in the early days of NATO.

"How much is that in real money?" There was no end to Little Lamar's curiosity.

"Real money?" answered Kleinschmidt.

"American money. What the fuck do you think he means, Lieutenant?" Lieutenant Colonel Rex King butted in on most conversations.

"Less than a penny, I suppose, Lamar." Kleinschmidt spent his junior year abroad in France.

"Hey, I've got almost a dollar. Maybe we could buy some hot water for the Major to shave with. Hey, maybe we could buy some and trade it for some of the parachutist's cigarettes."

Maybe Little Lamar wasn't all that dumb for a McNamara 1188.

"These yellow bastards are limitless Communists. They're not going to sell us any fucking hot water. Besides it wouldn't be right to make a profit off a fellow American."

"I don't know why not, King. King, that's the American way. Free enterprise, and all that. That's what you say we are fighting for."

"You're a dumb fuck, Sloan. Just you wait until you get back, just you wait. You and your friend Kleinschmidt will have a lot to answer for."

"I know, I know," answered Major John H. Sloan.

The staff at the Hanoi Hilton paid no attention to Article 55 or any of the other articles. Hot water was seldom poured. The prisoners suffered from the lack of an uninterrupted night's sleep. The beds were uncomfortable and the food strange. All the prisoners bitched a lot. Most of the prisoners, being American servicemen, resented the physical discomforts as much as their loss of freedom. After all they had given up large measures of freedom in exchange for admittance to the big PX. Even the lower ranking officers had once had comforts undreamed of by their captors. All the officers, at least the married ones, had electric can openers, color TVs, lots of radios, tape recorders, cars with gears operating automatically, automatic coffee makers, microwave ovens, electric bread warmers, power toothbrushes, houses that were air-cooled in the summer and heated centrally in the winter and the most modern and American of inventions--the electric barbecue grill, sold under the trade name Char-B- Queue by Hammacher-Schlemmer. The Char-B-Queue is infinitely thermostatically controlled, 1900 watts, available in black, avocado and turquoise, shipping weight 29 pounds, $59.95 (plus tax).

The men, all of them, the squids, the parachutists, the grunts, the jarheads, the spooks and if there were any high jumpers, the high jumpers would soon be checked out of the Hanoi Hilton. Their discomforts were about to end. Soon all would return to the big PX.

"Hello."

"Regina, this is Estelle Sloan. " Mrs. Sloan couldn't wait to hear the news of Mrs. King's visit with Mr. Nixon.

"Oh, hi, how are you Estelle?" Mrs. King put her gin and tonic down. She wedged the pink princess handset between her head and left shoulder and lit a filter tip low tar cigarette.

"Fine, fine. How are you? How was your trip? It is really too much."

"What trip?" Mrs. King was trying to blot the trip from her mind. Psychologists call it denial. Mrs. King was worried about what to do about Father McNaughton. Father McNaughton had bought her a ticket home on Southern Airways and paid for it with his American Express card. Should she pay him back? She had left her wig case in Ike Tapem's office. Ike Tapem doesn't work there anymore.

"What trip? You gotta be kidding. The most exciting trip anyone can possibly have. The greatest honor that one human being can bestow on another human being. And right in the oval office too." Mrs. Sloan thought highly of Mr. Nixon.

"I left my wig case there. Say, how was the meeting in LA? I wish I had gone. Why didn't you tell me?"

"I thought the computer did. I guess it knew that you were going to see President Nixon in the oval office."

"Say, you're going to be on TV tonight, aren't you? " Mrs. King wasn't going to talk about her Washington trip. Snooty, thought Mrs. Sloan. She wanted to hear about the trip in the worst way. It would give her something to tell her grandchildren.

"Yes, isn't it exciting. New Year's Eve with the POW wives."

"What are you going to wear?"

"My blue pants suit. But they've taped it already. They did it before Thanksgiving. I was so nervous."

"I just love your blue pants suit. " Mrs. King spilt some gin on the pink princess touchtone telephone. A large low tar ash dropped onto the shelf of her tummy.

"What do you mean about Thanksgiving? I didn't know they did a POW Thanksgiving show."

"They didn't. We made believe it was New Years Eve even though it was really Thanksgiving eve. They taped it."

"Suppose the asshole ended the war by New Years Eve?"

"Asshole?" That was the first time Mrs. Sloan had ever said that word aloud.

"Yeah, suppose Nixon ended the war before New Years? You wouldn't be a POW wife then, would you? The whole thing would have been a waste of time."

"I bet that is what the producer meant."

"What did he say, the producer?"

"He said, 'With my luck the asshole will end the war before this is in the can.' I didn't know what he meant." Asshole was said for the second time if quotes count.

"He meant that soon we will just be service wives and no one will give a shit about us." Mrs. King pulled hard on her gin and tonic water and spilt a little more.

"What's it going to be 1ike, I mean once they are home?"

"Hell."

"You know, I hate to say this, Regina, but these last six years, I mean with John a POW and all that have been the best I've had since high school. I'm ashamed to say it, but it is the truth. Don't tell anyone, but John's being a hero really saved our marriage. I really take pride in my husband--and Daddy too."

"You can trust Regina King. They (the POW years) would have been the happiest of my life, too, if only I'd had someone to fuck, they would have been the best ever." Poor Mrs. King's fucking had been nil these past six years.

"0h, I don't miss that at all. I mean having John do it to me. Ick, I hate it."

"You don't like to fuck?" Regina King really enjoyed fucking. "How can you even say that word? I don't like doing it at all. That's the best thing about it, not doing it. That and the way people treat you. Then there is Daddy. He is so proud of John. He's going to give us a lot next to his at the lake."

"Don't you want someone to hold you tight and make love? John's so much better looking than Rex and I sure would like a roll in the hay with Rex, would I ever. Sometimes I get so horny I just can't stand it. I just sit here and rub myself until I'm wet as can be."

"Regina, really. "

Both Dr. Kissinger and Le Duc Tho came to Paris a day early. Dr. Henry Kissinger came to Paris a day early just to dine at Lucas-Carton. Dr. Kissinger, by the way, is known in the trade as Henry the K. It makes him sound like a disk jockey, I know, but that is what they call him. Don't confuse the message with the messenger. Henry the K did indeed eat at Lucas-Carton. The good Doctor had sausages, which the menu called, "Saucissons chaud comme chez nous." Henry the K called them excellent.

"Just like ve have at our house. A little cold, but good."

He had a splendid bottle of Pommard ordered from the right side of the list. Whilst he ate, a dozen Secret Service men waited in the cold outside the door. A number of patrons didn't eat at that fine restaurant that night. Answering questions from Secret Service men puts one off ones food. It was said that both Mr. Lucas and Mr. Carton were upset. The wine steward winked and said, "Don't worry, it's been a good evening."

The whimsy of airline schedules brought Mr. Le Duc Tho to Paris a day early. If you think it is easy to book passage between Hanoi and Paris, just try it one time. Tho had to make a chancy connection out of Rawalpindi for Karachi, thence on to Baghdad for an Air France through flight to Paris. If he missed the flight out of Rawalpindi, it might be days and days before he could get out of Pakistan. Mrs. Le Duc Tho said, "Don't take any chances, Tho. Go a day early. You know what a bad temper Henry the K has. There is no telling what he might do."

Le Duc Tho thought what the heck, it might be nice to bum around Paris for the day and rest up from the long flight. The flight, including layovers and changes took 27 hours. Le Duc Tho traveled tourist class. Le Duc Tho thought tourists would be better advised to stay home or take a boat. He wandered around Paris and bought a couple of novels for Mrs. Le Duc Tho. He ended up far from the Madeleine on the Rue de Vaugirard and popped into an Indonesian restaurant. He had a bottle of Alsatian beer and the house speciality, a Rijsttafel. Le Duc Tho called it awful.

The next morning Henry the K took his Cadillac limousine to the North Vietnamese villa in Gif-sur-Yvette. The limousine had been flown from the United States of America in an Air Force C-141. C-141 is the name of a Lockheed cargo plane. It has been modified at great expense especially to carry Dr. Kissinger's limousine. Dr. Kissinger was making a house call on Le Duc Tho. It was January 8th, 1973 and the weather in Paris was cold. That didn't stop dozens of newsmen from following Kissinger's convoy on their motorcycles.

"How do you like our new place, Dr. Kissinger?" It was Le Duc Tho greeting Henry the K on the steps of the rented villa. He saw the Caddy and wished he had brought his bicycle.

"It is closer than Rambouillet, though not as historic..." Henry Kissinger had a sense of history. Indeed, he had taught Charles that subject at some school across the River from Boston.

"No Medicis." Mr. Le Duc Tho knew a thing or two about history himself.

"Quite."

The two statesmen went into the Villa Leger. Dr. Kissinger turned his face toward the cameras and tripped on the sill.

"Dear Henry, did you have a nice holiday?"

"Very nice, thank you. I went to Palm Springs. Wonderful weather. You should try it sometime, dear Tho. I stayed with some ambassador, a rich devil who is fond of TV actors. He has a grand house, his own golf course."

"I don't play golf." Le Duc Tho had never held a golf club in his life.

"Well, it was a relief from all these tedious trips. Say, how was your holiday, Le Duc Tho?"

"Oh, it would have been nice enough—I saw my grandchildren—if it hadn't been for all that bombing; I thought. He agreed, dear Henry, then I went home an almost got my ass killed. You simply ruined our house. Mrs. Le Duc Tho is most upset. It really was quite unnecessary. As men of honor, we should keep our word."

"Hell Tho, I did agree in good faith, I really did. It is that goddamn Thieu, he didn't like points three and four."

"You mean to say that you bombed my villa and killed God knows how many people because of Nguyen Van Thieu. Why?"

"As I say, he objected to points three and four. But honestly Tho, I didn't have anything to do with bombing your villa. It was those folks at AFOPs. I really am very sorry."

"Do you mean to say that you bombed us because Thieu objected to free elections?"

"That's about the size of it. Free elections are, I believe, covered by point number three."

"Why didn't you bomb him?"

"Dear Tho, you simply don't understand the American electorate."

"A bunch of, how do you Americans say it, dumb fucks if you ask me."

"Well, the President describes them as children."

"Be that as it may, let's get down to negotiating again." Mr. Tho thought the CIA must have slipped something in his morning coffee. Mr. Tho adored his grandchildren. He couldn't quite understand what was going on.

"That's why we're here," said Henry Kissinger.

"Got to earn our pay," said the man from the North. "Let us start then. "

"OK."

"There are several things, I'm sorry to say that are unacceptable to Thieu."

"Like what?"

"Well, as I said, there is this business about free elections."

"But we agreed to that way back in 1954 in Geneva and then again last October. I even have an unsigned memo from you, dear Dr. Kissinger. Don't you remember last October when you said, 'Peace is at hand.' Free elections are covered by point four, or if you say so, point three."

"I know and that's why we had to bomb you."

"I thought that you Americans believed in democracy."

"They do, they do, dear Tho."

"Then what's all this bombing, dear Henry? We agreed to all nine points and then, as you Americans say, you bombed the shit out of us."

"How true."

"What now, dear Henry?"

"Well, first there are the prisoners."

"Point three, Henry. You can have them back, dear Henry. We don't want them. They are a bunch of troublemakers if ever I've seen any. They are a real pain in the ass. You can have them, He don't want them. Please take them."

"Not our prisoners, that is to say the prisoners you hold, but the ones that we hold."

But we agreed, Doctor Kissinger, that all prisoners would be released within sixty days of the cease-fire."

"Thieu is not going to release any political prisoners, period."

"No free elections and no prisoners, eh?"

"That's about the size of it."

"But you said--"

"I know that. General Haig is talking to Thieu at this very moment, but it won't do any good. I believe elections and prisoners are covered by points three and four. We will have to change them both."

"But we agreed to free elections under international supervision. And you Americans are always talking about prisoners. I read the papers after all."

"Thieu says that he'd be out on his ass if there are free elections. The CIA, and I don't think I'm violating security, agrees with him. But you'll have to consider the source on that. In fact Thieu said that all nine points are just a clever CIA scheme to get him out of office. Surely you heard his two hour speech."

"You Americans are letting Nguyen Van Thieu wave the tail of the United States of America."

"How true."

"Well, I must insist on free elections and release of all prisoners of war. My God, Dr. Kissinger, you Americans are always talking about POWs and making the world free for democracy. I've seen your bumper sticker." Dr. Kissinger's limousine had a bumper sticker that said: SEND HOME OUR POWs. Henry Kissinger had not authorized such a sticker. I have not been able to determine who was responsible for sticking the bumper sticker on Dr. Kissinger's bumper.

"Well, Mr. Le Duc Tho, there ain't going to be any free elections in the South and Thieu is keeping the prisoners and that, dear boy, is that."

"Suppose we don't go along?"

"Then we are simply going to bomb you off the map. That Christmas business was just a sample. "

"And after that, what?"

"Ah, then we will have to make some concessions." Henry the K didn't win the Nobel Peace Prize by being intransigent.

"Then let us compromise now."

"Fine, OK with me. Where will we start?"

"Well, how about saying that there will be free elections and then not bother to hold them, just like in the Geneva accords."

"Thieu won't buy that; I tried."

"Then can't you come up with some pettifogging statement; you've done it so well in the past dear Henry."

"Done," said the Nobel Laureate."

"Now what about the political prisoners?"

"Thieu wants to keep them."

"Then we will keep your fliers."

"That won't wash. That is the one thing that would make Nixon use the bomb."

"You mean to say that your Mr. Nixon would destroy the world for 586 cowards?"

"He thinks of himself as a peacemaker and would indeed use the bomb to that end."

"Then you are welcome to them. Please take them or we will deliver them anywhere you say. We will pay for their tickets, first class if you want, Henry."

"Now you're talking. But it won't be necessary for you to pay for their tickets, it's all been worked out. Hey, it's getting late, what do you say about me buying you lunch? "

"You are my guest, Dr. Kissinger. But thank you just the same. You capitalists are always so generous."

"There is just one more little thing." Kissinger will have to use all of his skills as a negotiator on this one.

"And what is that?"

"It is about the size of the peace keeping force."

"Well, if it comes to bombing again, you can have all you want. That last bombing spree almost knocked out both of Hanoi Light and Power's power plants. We were without lights for over six hours one time and for almost five that last raid. No sense to bomb again, Henry. I'm reasonable. I mean you're going to keep all the political prisoners and there'll be no elections, so why not have a whole nation full of peace observers. I rather fancy having all those Poles and Hungarians around."

"Dear Tho, the problem is the Canadians. They only want to send 290 men. "

"Any number you want is OK with me, Henry. Now then, where shall we eat? I know this little place that the tourists have never heard of."

"In a minute, first...

"You have something else?"

"No, no, it's still the truce commission."

"As I say you can have as many as you like or as few. It makes no difference to me or my government."

"It seems that we can only muster 1160."

"Fine, fine. Now what about lunch? Would you like...?"

"Just a minute. I mean to say that Mr. Nixon would like for you to insist on 1160, while we hold out for 10,000. We'll give in, in the interests of peace. That way if the whole thing blows it will look like it was your fault."

"And then you'll start bombing us again."

"Dear Tho, how could you even think such a thing?"

"All right we agree to only 1160. You are in fact generous to give in to our demands, dear Henry. Now that that is settled how about some pressed duck? I know this little out of the way place that has delicious pressed duck."

"Ah."

"Perhaps you would prefer a Rijsttafel. I know this little place that's not too expensive. They have fine beer, Henry. I know that you Germans like beer."

"Just a minute. Let us finish our negotiating."

"But we have, haven't we?"

"First we will have to issue a statement that we agree on all points save the number of observers. Let me see, today is the 8th. We should have it all wrapped up by the 20th or 21st."

"But Henry we agree now, so why in the name of God should we wait? What with all those people dying and everything. Besides it must be very expensive for you dropping all those bombs."

"Mr. Nixon wants to delay until after he takes the oath of office for his second term. He says that he wants to bug the peace people."

"Your Mr. Nixon goes to a lot of trouble and expense just to bug people, doesn't he?

"If only you knew, dear Tho. You said something about pressed duck, what about the Tour d'Argent?"

"I don't wish to seem rude, dear Henry, but don't you think that the Tour d' Argent is a little pricey? "

"I'll buy."

"You are a very generous man, Doctor Kissinger."

On January 20th, 1973, Richard Milhous Nixon takes the oath of office for his second term as thirty-seventh President of the United States of America. He swears, "I, Richard Milhous Nixon, do solemnly swear that I will faithfully execute the office (execute the office?) of the President of the United States and will to the best of my ability, preserve, protect and defend the Constitution of the United States." That is what he swore, he really did. I will be willing to go before a notary and so state. Maybe that thing about the best of my ability takes the curse off Mr. Nixon's oath. Richard Nixon went on to say that he sees a new era of peace. The next day Lyndon Baines Johnson dropped dead. He thought of himself as the architect of the great society. He was wrong. Most people thought of him as the mad bomber. Lyndon Johnson didn't like Richard Nixon and Richard Nixon didn't like him.

Then the very next day, President Nixon announced that an accord had been reached in the Vietnamese war and that a cease-fire would begin on January 27th. After months of intractable negotiations the United States, in an act of supreme statesmanship, agreed to a UN peacekeeping force of 60 men. All prisoners of war would be freed within sixty days. This gave both sides four days to kill people and sixty days to release prisoners. Mr. Nixon said, "We have obtained peace with honor."

"The next day Henry Kissinger, Henry the K that is, said the ceasefire agreement guarantees political independence for the Saigon government. The Taiwanese give better guarantees on their Rolex Oysters. Henry the K went on to say, "Ve have obtained peace vith honor."

On January 25th, Lyndon Baines Johnson, the thirty-sixth President of the United States, is buried on the banks of the Pedernales River. Among the mourners are the thirty-seventh President, Richard Nixon and Major Roderick Vincent Wellborne, III.

Major Wellborne wears the gold aiguillettes of a presidential aide. Wellborne was receiving promotions with the speed of a General Haig. On January 26th, the Pentagon suddenly orders the end of the military draft. Henceforth the Army would make do exclusively with 1188s.

A lot of important things happened on January 27th, 1973.

That morning Le Duc Tho and William P. Rogers, the then Secretary of State, acting on the instructions of Henry the K, signed the Vietnam Peace Pact in Paris. The pact calls for fighting and bloodshed to end at midnight. Due to carelessness, or maybe the pressed duck, the Pact didn't define midnight. Has midnight Paris time, Washington time or Vietnamese time? The Pact didn't say. The agreement was further complicated by the fact that The Republic of Vietnam used Vietnamese Peoples

Standard and the United States Military used Military Time. The two times differ by one hour, with Vietnamese Peoples Standard Time being one hour earlier than the American's time. As far as Henry Kissinger is concerned, it is a good thing that the Nobel Peace Prize Committee does not take into account clerical correctness in awarding the Nobel Peace Prize. As far as Lieutenant Colonel William B. Nolde of Mount Pleasant, Michigan was concerned, the oversight was a bad thing. He was killed by an artillery shell shortly before midnight Vietnamese Peoples Standard Time. The Nobel Prize Committee tried to give Le Duc Tho the Nobel Peace Prize. Le Duc Tho asked, "How could I, in good conscience, accept the Nobel Peace Prize?" The Prize was given to Henry the K, who didn't ask any questions. The prize is a gold medal and $250,000.00 in American money. Dr. Kissinger made a very gracious acceptance speech in which he said, "Thank you."

He's so well mannered; Dr. Kissinger would not say what use, if any, was made of the money. Le Duc Tho didn't tell Mrs. Le Duc Tho that he turned down $ 250,000.00. She would, as he said, "Have a Hissy."

As far as it can be determined the last American bombs were dropped by Marine Air Group 12 just short of midnight Military Time. Marine Air Group 12 was commanded by Colonel Dean Macho. That is his name, honest to God it is. I could never make a name like that up. In honor of the occasion all the bombs on the Marines' last mission were painted red, white and blue. Each bomb contained 500 pounds of napalm. One bomb was inscribed: "500 pounds of Jelly Beans, Care Package." The last bomb was dropped by First Lieutenant Thomas Boykin. The bomb read: "This bomb is dedicated to the hope that all the Marines here at Bien Hoa will soon be enjoying a Good and Everlasting PIECE (sic). "

The sic is mine. For those of you who do not believe this, I assure you Time Magazine would not lie.

■■■

The last bomb burned up three houses and all the people in those houses. There was quite a celebration at the officers club at the Bien Hoa Marine Air Base that night. The pilot, First Lieutenant Thomas Boykin, I am told, offered this toast: "Here's to peace with honor. " It has never been determined with any accuracy the names of all the people in those three houses.

The purpose of all prisons from the Hanoi Hilton to the Federal Minimum Security Prison down in Montgomery, Alabama-- and even Leavenworth--is not to reform prisoners or even just keep them. The purpose of all prisons is to make prisoners appear contrite. Smart prisoners know this and are contrite. Those that don't are in for a bad time indeed. Repentance must be conspicuous. George Jackson said it well: "No one walks with his head up. No one will leave this place (San Quentin, a prison in California) until they can see that thing in their eyes. Resignation, defeat, it must be clearly stamped across the face." George Jackson, not stamped with that look, never left San Quentin alive.

When the prisoners at the Hanoi Hilton were told of their parole, they were very happy. After prison the Big PX seems like a very good thing. The parachutists, especially the parachutists that collaborated on film and radio, changed their colors back to red, white and blue. They hadn't been traitors. They had the instinct for survival. They were contrite. They had that look in their eyes. That look left once they heard about the peace with honor. The former Petains and Quislings now taunted their captors all the time. The worst offender, the rudest of all was Lieutenant Colonel Rex King. For example, he said to Nguyen Thanh Linh, "You Godless Commie bastard, Nixon will get you yet. He'll dial your number, you fucking Godless Commie bastard." The majority of the POWs went on as before. They weren't quite sure the Big PX was at hand. The guards were puzzled by the rude behavior of their former friends, but they took the ill manners with considerable grace.

The North Vietnamese were as glad to have the war over as the prisoners were. Some say they were even gladder. They were happy, we know that. The manager of the Hanoi Hilton expressed his joy by or-ganizing a small entertainment. Now in a prison camp a real entertainment is seldom seen, but there in the courtyard of the Hoa Lo prison was an entertainment. The sandbag engine house served as the stage. There were singers and dancers and acrobats and jugglers and magicians and musicians and girls, beautiful girls. Colonel King turned his back and refused to look. Nguyen Thanh Linh pointed at him and laughed. Then the prisoners had a feast and what a feast it was.

They were served meat--chicken, duck and water buffalo. So much meat, there was at least a half of a pound per prisoner. And then there was rice, not the usual soggy brown rice, but pure white tasty rice. The prisoners developed a taste for rice over the years and mightily enjoyed the refined rice. And then there were vegetables: red cabbage, sweet potatoes, squash and pickled Russian cucumbers. And fruit, lots of fruit, there were piles of bananas and stacks of breadfruit and canned Romanian peaches. There were Chinese gumdrops and pots of tea. And, glory of glories, there was a package of Dienbienphu cigarettes for each prisoner--factory made cigarettes and not too strong, wherein comes the name Dienbienphu. And the grandest treat of all, and much to the regret of Sloan's liver, was three liter bottles of Hanoi beer for each man. Real beer and damn good beer it was.

The prisoners were astonished at the treatment. No prison had ever been like this. Maybe they really were going to go home. As the guards and cooks' boys laid the food on, the prisoners looked on in wonderment and then tucked it in. They ignored the chopsticks and the Vietnamese custom of never touch-ing food with ones left hand. The left hand in Vietnam is re-served for the wiping of ones ass. The guards shook their heads in disbelief. They thought the Americans were indeed barbarians.

Sloan, glad as he was to see the food, was overjoyed at the Hanoi beer. He lusted after more. He said to Rex King, "Colonel King, I'll swap you my gum drops for your beer."

"And your peaches." Rex King loved peaches. He never drank beer.

"Done."

So Sloan had six liters of beer. Kleinschmidt had some cannabis--Hanoi Gold. Kleinschmidt traded some of his stash to one of the CIA pilots in exchange for his three bottles of beer and gave them to Sloan. So Sloan had nine liters of beer. Nine liters of beer is a lot of beer. Sloan got a little tight--a peek at the future, maybe. It was a fine party, best in years.

The Long Binh Prison was called the Long Binh Prison. No irony in that name. Long Binh is beyond irony. Naming it after the George Cinq in Paris or the Hamounia in Harrakech somehow doesn't do. The Long Binh George Cinq. The Long Binh Hamounia. The Long Binh Ritz. The Long Binh Hilton. None of them quite work. It was the Long Binh Prison outside the South Vietnamese city of Danang.

The record keeping at the Long Binh Prison was shoddy, shoddy like the rooms. No records were kept at all. That's not quite true, there was something called a head count. The Military Police knew how many prisoners they thought they had. They kept count by compound. They called the count a head count. Head count for Compound Number I, 875. Head count for Compound II, 976. And so forth. The counts weren't all that accurate, as some of the prisoners heads were counted twice. Some heads weren't counted at all.

The first few weeks of peace were absolute hell for all at Long Binh. Hell for the guards, hell for the prisoners. The guards were being worked to death separating the political pris-oners from what the United States Army called the real prisoners. They had it the wrong way around. The real prisoners were called Group A and they were going home. The political prisoners were called Group B and they weren't going home. The Group B were bound for the Isles de Poulo Condore in the South China Sea. Bad place, the Isles de Poulo Condore. It was no easy task, sorting out all those Group Bs from the Group A's. The guards complained a lot. The slang word for this is bitched. Well, the soldiers bitched at the extra work. They did have a lot of extra work to do. And hard work it was, seeing how the prison authorities didn't know the prisoners' names or their ranks or their branches of service or their occupations or where they were from or their political beliefs. A German with a riding crop would have been a great help.

The American officer in charge of all this sorting out was a military Police General by the name of Opel, John Opel. General Opel, skilled as he was in handling prisoners of war, couldn't handle this job. There were simply too many prisoners to be sorted in too short a time. General Opel didn't get to be a general by doing the job with the folks at hand. He used the old bureaucratic trick of always insisting on more people and a larger organization when there was anything that actually had to be done. That was the way to the general's stars. Old habits don't change especially when a man gets to be a general. General Opel requested 250 more Prisoner Interrogation Officers (PIOs) from the Commanding General in Saigon. Now the general in Saigon--I forget his name; what was it, Eastmorland--didn't get to be the top fighting general in the only war the Army had for nothing. He didn't come to the top of his trade by giving in to every MP general that came along. He said, "General Opel, goddamn it, perhaps you're not familiar with the peace agreement. We are taking our troops out of this shitass country just as fast as we can. The party's over and done with. No more war. So don't give me any more shit about PIOs. Is that clear, General Volkswagen? "

"But, General..." General Opel was tugging at his ear trying to think of something worth saying.

"I said I can't bring in any extra interrogation officers. The fucking White House would blow a fuse. Haig himself said, "No more PIOs."

"But General, I can't separate out all the Group Bs without interrogation officers. What if we sent a political prisoner north with the Group As? Think of the political consequences. I mean, General, we're dealing with Commies."

"You're right there, General Porsche."

"Can't you do something? Get me some civilian contractors or spooks or something."

"That's a thought. Meanwhile get cracking with the men you have."

"It takes hours just to interview just one of the yellow bastards. These boys (the prisoners) are hardened to the usual, er, ah, interrogation techniques." The usual interrogation techniques were not the rack or the bastinado or the iron maiden or the garrote or the Chinese Hater treatment or bamboo splinters driven under the fingernails and set on fire. To be sure the spooks at the CIA dropped prisoners out of their helicopters from time to time as an example for the rest of the prisoners.

They only wanted to make the prisoners appear contrite. George Jackson wouldn't have lasted long at Long Binh.

The usual interrogation technique used by the Military Police is called ringing up. When Major General Opel said in-interrogation technique, he meant ringing up. The Army has a lot of telephones called Double E-8s. Double E-8s are a common field telephone and are used by United States Army wherever they go. The Double E-8 has a magneto. The magneto makes the bell at the other end ring. The magneto is run by turning a crank. The faster the crank is turned, the louder the bell at the other end rings. It is a matter of electricity. If the wires are attached to a human being rather than to a bell, I am given to understand that it hurts. The faster the crank turns, the more it hurts.

The attachment of the wires is dictated by the perversion and ingenuity of the individual PIOs. The Military Police Corps does not attract compassionate people. General Opel often speaks of the American fighting men's ingenuity with a good deal of pride. Ingenuity or no ingenuity, the Double E-8 is a very cheap and very efficient piece of epistemological machinery. Each prisoner at the Long Binh Prison hoped that the bell wouldn't toll for him. "Can't you speed it up?" General Southmorland liked to make suggestions and ask questions.

"We're cranking them out as fast as we can. We can't turn them out any faster without more PIOs or at least some new guidelines" When General Opel said "guidelines" he sounded exactly like George Wallace, sneer and all. "New guide lines. That's a good point. I'll check out some new guide lines." He didn't get the guidelines out of some library; he called Ellsworth Bunker. Ellsworth Bunker called General Haig in Washington. General Haig called Nguyen Van Thieu in Saigon. Nguyen Van Thieu said, "If they can walk and are healthy, then they are Group B, political prisoners."

"Right," said General Haig.

General Opel, when informed of the new guidelines said,

"Shit, that's easy. They're all Group As, every last one of the yellow sons-a-bitches. I'll send them all home. No need wasting time ringing them up."

"What do you mean, they're all Group As? Clarify." General Northmorland frequently needed to have things clarified.

"In my thirty-two years as a member of the Military Police Corps, I have never seen a more disgraceful group of prisoners. Why the slant eyed fuckers have every disease known to man, save anthrax and small pox, and some of them had small pox before I got hold of them."

"You're saying you can't use health as a guideline."

"That's what I'm saying, General--General--er, Morland."

"I'll get more specific guidelines and get right back to you, General Mercedes."

To save time a general on the staff of Henry the K called General Opel direct from the White House. I'm told an edited verbatim transcript shows these words: "If they're missing something, then they are Group A. Eyes don't count, unless they're both gone. Ears don't count at all. All the rest are Group B."

"Jesus," said Admiral St. Thomas More when he listened to the original tape of this conversation.

The day of repatriation dawned at last. It dawned on February 5th, 1973, just 15 days after Henry the K told William Rogers to sign the Peace Pact in Paris. Now 15 days is not a long time, as General Opel will tell you. But to the 586 Ameri-can prisoners those 15 days lasted years. Rumor had it that today was the day, the day for the first 120 prisoners to start home. All the prisoners were made to get up at four in the morning. Believe it or not, many prisoners bitched about the early hour.

The prisoners assembled in the courtyard of the Hanoi Hilton. They were made to form in alphabetical order. They waited for a long time. It was just like being in the Army. The prisoners shifted from foot to foot as they waited; each trying to claim a small bit of the prison courtyard as his own. The order of the alphabet required Lieutenant Colonel Rex King to stand next to Second Lieutenant Justin Kleinschmidt.

"Watch your step, you Shavetail son of a bitch."

"Up yours, King. "

And so they waited.

Nguyen Thanh Linh was chosen to deliver the farewell address. Nguyen Thanh Linh climbed up on the top of the former sandbag engine house and started evangelizing. If there is one thing that Communists have in common with Christians, Republicans, vegetarians, prohibitionists and women libbers, it is their inability to resist saying a few words about their cause, no matter how inappropriate the occasion might be. To propagandize is human; to ignore is divine. Nguyen Thanh Linh looked as human as can be. The tunic he wore was so large at the neck. On his head rested a drab olive-colored elephant hat. He looked like an Asian gun bearer for a white hunter. The prisoners would be surprised when they found that Nguyen Thanh Linh not only spoke English, but he spoke it so very nicely. He spoke, "It is my duty to inform you all that as a concession to the United States of America, we are going to temporarily halt the peoples' struggle for a democratic government in all of Vietnam. In accordance with the agreement signed with your government and with the illegal government in Saigon, all of the regular militia of the Democratic People's Republic are to be released. Your government is not releasing what they call political prisoners. Your government is not releasing even senior members of the

People's Provisional Home Guard (PPHG). As a gesture of friendship, all of you gentlemen will be released."

A great shout went up. The parachutists started hugging and slapping the back of whoever happened to be standing next to them. The alphabet determined whom they slapped.

"Silence," ordered Nguyen Thanh Linh. He continued to speak in first rate English, ruined only by the odd extra diphthong or two. "I had not intended to give you a political les-son (the heck he didn't). It seems most of you all haven't grasped the nature of our struggle. I feel it incumbent on me to repeat the words of Ho Chi Minh. Uncle Ho sent these words to your Ambassador Harriman some years ago: 'When I was a young man and the Chinese controlled our nation, I fought the Chinese. When the French defeated the Chinese and controlled our nation, I fought the French. When the Japanese conquered the French and controlled our nation, I fought the Japanese. When you Americans defeated the Japanese, I hoped for freedom, but instead the French returned. I fought the French. The people conquered the French and the Americans returned. Now we are fighting you. The Americans will leave our country someday. We will fight anyone who tries to take our freedom.' Gentlemen, the war is not over just because you all are going home."

The prisoners stood in silence.

"According to the terms of the agreement, your government has provided a list of the order in which you all will return home."

The first name was John H. Sloan. The list was an odd mixture of high-ranking officers and long-term lower ranking prisoners. The unnamed prisoners outwardly envied the named ones and muttered amongst themselves. The look in their eyes was that of a wronged wife. Sad or mad, wait they must. There were simply too many prisoners to go home on a single day. The chosen parachutists went into an ecstasy and began speaking the tongues of the astronauts.

The last named was Kleinschmidt. The Vietnamese, with a humor unlike them, got his rank wrong. They called him a captain. Sloan wasn't sure, but he thought they might have called him a colonel. Surprised at hearing his name called first, he didn't hear his rank. Besides, he knew he was a major and Kleinschmidt was the lowest ranking Judge Advocate General in the Army. He was worried: Why was his name called first?

"Well, Major, looks like we are going home."

"So I gather, Littlesmith."

"I'm glad we're going home together, going home first."

"First in peace, last in war, hey."

"The last shall be first and the first last."

"Look Littlesmith, we've got some rough road ahead of us."

"It can't be rougher than the old Hilton. "

"You ever been in Leavenworth, son? "

The two men, prisoners for six years, were going home at last. They were both frightened.

Little Lamar was going home on the first load and so was Rex King. They and all the homeward bound wore new blue trousers, light blue shirts, new brown belts and black shoes. They wore light grey-green windbreakers and they were new. Everything was new, including royal blue flight bag. It was the sort of bag soldiers used to call an AWOL bag. The 120 were quite the best-dressed prisoners being repatriated that day. Buses, six buses carried them to Gia Lam Airport. They drove through downtown Hanoi, past both power plants of the old Hanoi Light and Power, past the Bac Hi Hospital and the Hanoi central Terminus and the flower market and the Jesuit Church and Le Duc Tho's villa and the Hanoi waterworks. Destruction was everywhere. Hanoi looked like the South Bronx.

At Gia Lam Airport a table had been set up. The terminal building, long since bombed flat, offered no protection from the light misty rain. A canopy made from an olive drab parachute served that need. I don't know where the North Vietnamese got the parachute, but it looked like United States Government property to me. A low wrought iron fence surrounded and defined the area under the parachute. At the table sat Lieutenant Colonel Nguyen Phuong and Colonel James B. Bennett. Colonel Bennett is a full bird colonel.

The three C-14ls were parked about 75 yards away. The landing strip had been repaired at enormous expense just so the C-141s could land that day.

As each prisoner's name was called, he stepped into the enclosure and in a move signifying repatriation walked past the table. Some of the prisoners, now ex prisoners saluted as they passed Colonel Bennett, some did not. A separate EOD officer met each man and escorted him to the Lockheed plane. Sloan watched it all. He was going on the third plane, another mix-up. He looked at the EOD officers and shook his head and wished for a cigarette. "Shit, Littlesmith, all of us are going to get it. They got a guard for each and every one of us, even for the gung-ho fly boys; we don't stand a chance."

Lieutenant Colonel King's Xerox copy slipped him a small piece of white canvas. As King King walked to the giant plane, he held it up for all to see. It read: GOD BLESS NIXON.

The Group Ks were to boat home across the Thach Han River. Major General John Opel was in charge of their repatriation. The peacekeeping force was in place, observing the exchange. Le Duc Tho would have been pleased if he could have seen all those Poles and Hungarians. Most all of the 290 Canadians were watching. The prisoners were trucked to the exchange point in General Motors trucks. The motors are not generals, they are just called that. The trucks were the standard Army truck and they were called 6 by 6s. The trucks had five tires on each side plus two spare tires. This makes ten tires or even twelve tires if one counts the spares. Why the trucks were called 6 by 6s is just another one of the mysteries of Detroit. Detroit has many mys-teries. General Opel, who really is a general, had the trucks stop behind a slight rise in the land some 100 yards from the river. General Opel called this distance 100 meters, but it was closer to 100 yards. Opel wanted to protect the 6 by 6 in case war broke out during the exchange. Attention to details is another way to the general's stars.

One peace observer, a man from Calgary, came up to General Opel and said, "Can't you bring those trucks closer, sir?" "No," answered General Opel.

"But General, most of those men are crippled and can't walk 100 yards on one leg."

"Fuck 'em. Let 'em hop," said Major General John Opel.

The men from the North were not allowed to bring one single thing with them save the clothes they wore. All were issued clean prison uniforms in honor of this historic day. Before the prisoners left Long Binh they were made to strip naked, leave all of their belongings behind and take a shower. The shower was like a car wash--in one side and out the other. On the other side each prisoner was given a body search, including what the PIOs called a fingerwave. For the benefit of those readers who have managed to avoid prison and the Military Police Corps, it should be pointed out that a fingerwave is a rectal inspection. After the fingerwave, the prisoners were issued clean prison uniforms. No attempt was made to match the size of the uniform with the size of the man. Whatever else the prisoners had was abandoned at the entrance to the car wash. Not that they had all that much to discard after the long years in prison. All that was left for confiscation were a few photographs of a parent or of a child or of a wife, or perhaps, of a girlfriend. A letter or two, maybe. An address book. Not much. Whatever they had was left outside the showers at Long Binh Prison.

As the prisoners, now the former prisoners, crossed the Thach Han in those tiny boats they took off the clean uniforms and threw them into the river.

"Fucking yellow perverts," shouted Major General John Opel as he shook his fist at the Thach Han River.

The Lockheed C-l4ls Here especially modified for the task of bringing home the prisoners from Gia Lam International Airport. And what planes they were. The front halves were decorated exactly like a first class cabin on an Eastern Air Lines DC-10. The rear half of each C-141 was fitted out as a flying hospital: operating theater, recovery room, X-ray department, intensive care unit complete with cardiac monitors and all, nurses station, wards for the junior men and private rooms for the general grade officers. The plane was a feat of American technology if ever you've seen one. The Pentagon believed its own press releases and was taking no chances, lest anything happened to the POWs on their way home.

After all, a long and quite expensive war had been fought just to get these men back.

Major John H. Sloan was the first man to board the third plane. He nodded as he passed Colonel John B. Bennett, sitting with his North Vietnamese counterpart. His EOD officer, Lieutenant Colonel Gerald Witherspoon, met him just outside the low wrought iron fence. He grasped Sloan firmly and led him to the plane. "Everyone in the States knows what you've done."

"Holy shit," answered Sloan. It was going to be worse than ever he thought. If the whole country knew the details of his surrender, a fair trial would be impossible.

They entered the huge plane and turned left towards the first class section. Sloan glanced toward the hospital and spot-ted an examining table graced with a full set of surgical cutlery. He focused on a hypodermic syringe suitable for a horse and be-lieved the worst. "Jesus Christ, we're going to get it right on the plane. "

"He'll give you whatever the doctors will allow."

"Could I sit down?" Sloan thought he was going to pass out. His skin had no color. He needed to speak to Kleinschmidt. If he sat by the door at least he could see him as he passed. Unless, of course, they took him to the right.

"Anything you say," said Lieutenant Colonel Witherspoon. In spite of his name, Gerry Witherspoon was a fairly faithful copy of Sloan. Colonel Witherspoon had pinched three one-tenth-liter bottles of medical brandy on the flight down from Clark. Anything for the POWs. Sloan interpreted Witherspoon's good nature as an interrogator's ploy. True, he sniffed the brandy, but that could be another trick. Good old Witherspoon had no way of knowing that Sloan believed himself on the way to Leavenworth and that the Army was gathering additional evidence in direct violation of his Fifth Amendment rights. Witherspoon believed Sloan's palsy and dilated eyes and ashen skin were the result of ill treatment at the hands of the North Vietnamese. What those savages did to our boys.

Colonel Witherspoon thought about not allowing Sloan to sit where he pleased. Each seat had been assigned in advance. That is the way real airlines do it on deluxe flights. The Air Force often mimicked the real airlines. On each man's seat sat the man's three-part REPAK file and comfort kit. Witherspoon had been in-structed by Dr. Roger Shield to be firm, but flexible. Witherspoon decided to be flexible. He let Sloan sit by the door. He sent one of the nurses to get Sloan's REPAK fie and comfort kit.

Nurses were being used as stewardesses and wore special uniforms. The United States Air Force has what amounts to stewardesses and they are called flight attendants. The flight attendants are en-listed women and are quite frankly, to paraphrase General George S. Brown, a bit dowdy. It is unkind to say, but in truth the flight attendants were female 1188s. Air Force nurses acted as surrogate flight attendants. The surrogates were chosen by the IBM 360/65. The computer paid particular attention to the nurses' good looks and tits. And I must say it picked some very pretty nurses indeed. They were Marilyn Chambers, Ivory Snow sort of women.

"Littlesmith," Was Sloan ever glad to see Kleinschmidt. He was very nervous and seeing Kleinschmidt cheered him a bit.

"Major Sloan."

"Sit down here."

Captain Tom Gilliam wasn't sure what he should do. Klein-schmidt was supposed to sit in 14B, not by some aging officer.

In 14B rested Kleinschmidt's two-part REPAK file and his comfort kit. Captain Gilliam had paid little attention to Dr. Roger Shield's briefings and had no idea what to do. Gilliam looked around for help and caught the eye of Colonel Witherspoon. Wither- spoon gave a nod. The nod in nod language meant be flexible.

"Jesus, Littlesmith, it's worse than we ever thought. They've got us with one-on-one guards. And wait till you see the stuff they gave me. It is crazy. Maybe this is some trick and we're not really going home."

"Oh, it's probably CIA. They love to make big deals."

"They're a bunch of kids, playing at James Bond."

Come to think of it, the C-141 did look like something out of a James Bond movie. "Say what is your guard like? Mine is a real flake. All he talks about is Yale and Mory's. He's a dummy, a Harvard man most likely."

"What did you tell him?"

"That I wasn't talking until I speak to my lawyers. The fucker just laughed."

"Did you see all that stuff they have in the back?"

"Yeah, it looks like the CIA station in Saigon."

"Littlesmith, it looks like they are going to do more than just ring us up. "

"Look Major, it is only fair to warn you. I mean, I don't know what you're going to do when the bell tolls for thee, but when it tolls for me, I'm talking. I can't stand pain. If it comes to ringing me up, then I'll tell them the whole thing, I mean about pissing and everything."

"Thanks for telling me that, but I think I will try to hold out as long as I can. I guess I've just got more to lose than you."

All the other passengers were solemn, very solemn. Sloan and Kleinschmidt were the only ones talking and they were whispering. As long as the thing was on the ground it could be called a whisper jet. The crew of nurses and the EOD officers grew nervous. To break the gloom, the Marilyn Chamberses came down the aisle and handed out copies of Playboy and the Far Eastern edition of Stars and Stripes.

The door of the great tacky plane clanked shut. The engines revved up. The large combination flying hospital and all first class airliner turned off the parking ramp and lumbered down the runway. The pilot, one of the President's own pilots from the air wing of the White House, gave the plane full throttle. One of the parachutists yelled, "Pour the coal to it!" With that the parachutists whooped and shouted and yelled and cheered. What a din. It is enough to make a man shout with joy, when he knows he is going home at last. Going home after all those years of hardship. Going home, going home.

Sloan and Kleinschmidt weren't sure where they were going. It was bound to be some prison. They were merely in transit, bound for another prison. They watched in wonder as the parachutists and a couple of grunts jumped and shouted and slapped and hugged each other like football players after a goal. Then, as the plane banked over the flooded Red River delta, a thought leaped into the buggers' heads. Here is that thought: they were returning to the real world of heterosexuality. In that world homosexuality or at least the appearance of homosexuality is for-bidden. The parachutists grabbed the nurses. Some were quite rough and some of the nurses quite delicate. The nurses took the mauling in all good humor. They had been briefed to expect such behavior by the diligent staff of EGRESS RECAMP. Someone on Dr. Shield's staff had the unusual foresight to order and issue girdles manufactured by the Italian firm of Campi, Fermand Sons. This fine old firm field tested their products on the streets of Naples. The nurses that didn't wear their Fermi girdles had good reason to wish they had.

Sloan read the lead article in the Stars and Stripes. The paper thought the ex-POWs were going to receive a Sergeant York welcome. The paper could be a plant. This was a time for suspicion. In the brochure part of his REPAK file Sloan found orders promoting him to full bird colonel. The summary of pay due him amounted to the American dream come true. He had over $100,000.00 coming to him. And if that isn't the American dream, goddamn it, I would like to know what is. Further there was a note saying that Congress passed a law forgiving all the POWs of their income tax. Sloan couldn't help but wonder what they did for the men that chose death rather than surrender. Nothing.

Colonel Witherspoon came along and said, "Colonel Sloan, how ya'doing?"

"Fine, thank you."

"You will be expected to make a few off the cuff comments once we get to Clark."

"I've nothing to say."

"The EGRESS RECAP staff considered that possibility and has prepared a statement for you."

"Listen, I'm not signing a thing. You can ring me up, but I ain't signing nothing."

"No, no, not for you to sign, for you to read. That is to say for you to when you get off the plane. You will be first man off the plane."

Colonel Witherspoon handed Sloan a 3 by 5 card and here is what the card said: "1: We have been honored and privileged to serve you, my fellow Americans, as POWs. We are profoundly grateful to our Commander in Chief, Richard Nixon, for bringing us home with honor. God bless Nixon. God bless America."

"What can you make of this, Littlesmith "?

"Jesus, what's going on? No, don't say it. You can't say it."

"You're right. They're trying to make a fool of me."

"Don't say it, Major. "

"What can I do?"

General King's C-141 arrived in the Philippines before Sloan's. His flickering image was seen by tens of millions of Americans from San Diego to Caribou, Maine. Live television coverage of this event substituted for the regular entertainment. Here is what those tens of millions of Americans saw:

•Long shot of C-141 touching down. Slowly zoom in for 15 seconds.

•Cut to official greeting committee.

•Zoom in on Admiral Noel Arthur Meredyth Gayler. Admiral Gayler starts to pick his nose.

•Quick cut to Lieutenant General William G. Moore, Jr.

•Pan to First Sergeant Solomon Kalona. Kalona yawns. At first glance Kalona looks like the doorman at the Berlin Hilton or perhaps a Spanish Admiral. It is hard to tell.

•Quick cut to Colonel Roderick Vincent Wellborne III. Colonel Wellborne wears the gold aiguillettes of a Presidential Aide.

•Fade to the C-141.

• Tight shot of General King grinning.

• Zoom out, showing General King holding his GOD BLESS NIXON sign.

• Pan cheering crowds. Crowd is hysterical.

• Zoom in on a sign in the crowd saying: Welcome Home Mabuhay. The viewers remain ignorant of who or what a Mabuhay is.

•Pan crowd to GOD LOVES NIXON sign.

•Fade to King shaking hands with Admiral Gayler.

•Pan as General King shakes hands with other dignitaries.

•Focus on Kalona's face. He smiles.

•Cut to crowds.

•Cut back to General King standing in front of a battery of microphones.

•Zoom in as General King says: "It has been our privilege and distinct honor to serve you Americans. At no time during my imprisonment did I fail to support my President and my President's policy. Thank you President Nixon for bringing us home with honor on our feet, instead of our knees. God bless Nixon. God bless America."

•Switch to the White House. President Nixon sits in a large wing chair beside a cheery fire and watches General King on a large color television set. Mr. Nixon has a large Beefeaters gin sitting on the floor by his side. It is out of sight of the viewers, however.

• Tight shot of President Nixon smiling. The President speaks: "This is the most moving experience I've had since I was at the--while I've been in the White House--in this President's whole life."

• Network difficulties. The sound and picture are lost. Tens of millions of Americans from San Diego to Caribou, Maine wonder if their television sets are broken. Most of those Americans get up from their chairs or off their couches and try to adjust the fine-tuning.

• Switch to Washington studio. Regina King is being interviewed by Walter Cronkite. Why the vast resources of CBS chose Regina King I find difficult to understand. The only explanation that comes to mind: CBS anchormen are as fallible as Ike Tapem, whom you will remember, we left clutching the iron bars outside the White House and swearing vengeance. To the best of my memory here is what Cronkite said:

Mr. Cronkite: The whole world watches with profound pleasure the return of these brave men. It is a re-creation of Concord, Antietam, The Alamo, Bellow Woods and the flag raising at Iwo Jima. This is truly an historic day. Mrs. King , you must be very proud of your husband and the moving statement of his. Your husband has been a prisoner for a long time . How do you think he looked?

Mrs. King: He looked gorgeous.

Mr. Cronkite: I am sure you were delighted to see your husband, but we, the American people, are wondering how healthy he looked. How he must have suffered during those long years in a communist prison. Just how did he look, healthwise?

Mrs. King: Oh, he looked better than I've ever seen him.

Mr. Cronkite: You mean to say that your husband looked healthier now than he did six years ago before he was a POW?

Mrs. King: That's what I mean to say. The bags under his eyes are gone. His skin looks clear. He's lost some of his pot.

Mr. Cronkite: President Nixon has taken great personal interest in the POWs. Mrs. King, you have met with Mr. Nixon and talked with him about the POWs. What do you think of Mr.Nixon? What kind of a man is he?

Mrs.King: President Nixon is an asshole.

•Cut to Burger King commercial. Staccato voices sing, "Have it your way, have it your way."

The network difficulties cleared up in time for Sloan's arrival at Clark Field. And what a spectacular arrival it was. The hard, stiff shock absorbers on the military jet allow it to land at a much greater speed than say a DC-10 whisper jet. The C-141 slammed down on the tarmac and the pilot simultaneously hit the thrust reversers. Thrust reversers reverse thrust. I have no idea how they work. The proper verb for turning on one

of these thrust reversers is hit. Well, the pilot hit the thrust reversers and the Brodibingnagian jet almost hit its nose. The monster was making 50 knots as it came to the exit ramp. The President's pilot locked the brakes and cut engines number 3 and 4. The great jet whipped to the right. It scared the shit out of the dignitaries. "Scare the shit out of" is just an expression. It is commonly used by soldiers and sailors. It is used on this page simply for effect and is not intended to imply that any of the dignitaries actually had a bowel movement, ever. There was no reason for the dignitaries fear. The pilot was competent and no more reckless than most pilots. The plane came to a stop on the exact spot prescribed by the unit director of the network television pool. The exact spot was a little closer than the dignitaries would have liked.

Sloan stepped off the jet into the glare of the klieg lights. He was greeted by Admiral Noel A.H. Gayler, Commander in Chief, Pacific, or CINCPAC, as it is known in the trade. Please remember what CINCPAC is. There is a doggerel about old

CINCPAC which is only of passing interest to this narrative. Here it is:

Admiral Gayler, a sailor

gay, sailor

sailor, gayler

Admiral Gayler is a sailor.

The Admiral Gayler welcomed Sloan, as did General Moore and Sergeant Kalona. The sergeant is the head boy of all the Army enlisted Enlisted men include drafted persons. The greetings of these anonymous men were another event in a very strange day. Colonel Wellborne took Sloan's hand and said, "The whole nation is proud of what you have done." Colonel Wellborne wears the gold aiguillettes of a Presidential aide.

"Because I've been squirming for awhile and refuse to sign anything?"

"The President sends his warm personal regards."

"He does?"

Colonel Wellborne motioned for Sloan to step in front of the forest of microphones, into the path of the video camera. The light on the video camera winked red. Sloan, trapped in the dark woods like a deer in a poacher's light, froze. The terror in his eyes was that of a horse in a burning stable. He realized, re-alized slowly at first, that all these people were waiting for his statement. He wasn't going to give it, period. He stood terrified, rooted, and dumb.

Admiral Noel A.M. Gayler, CINCPAC, coughed and nervously motioned to the EOD Admiral. The EOD Admiral sought the aid of one of the EGRESS RECAMP public relations men. The public relations man had a direct line to the unit director of the network television pool. The public relations man said "Turn on another fucking camera, you dumb shit. " Someone paid to fool the public is called a public relations man.

The red light blinked off. The public relations man went up to Sloan and whispered in his left ear. I don't know what he said and Sloan doesn't remember. Sloan nodded and pretty soon the red light returned. This is what Sloan said: "I have been a soldier most of my life. During that time, I have always tried to fulfill my obligations to my country and to my uniform. I failed in my obligations. I am sorry. No soldier can be proud of the fact that he was a prisoner of war. We hardly fulfilled our obligations by surrendering. We will carry the guilt to our graves. Why did so many brave young men die, while the cowards lived? That question will haunt the soldier down all the days of his life. The prisoner of war will know the answer to the final question: did I do my duty? I can only say in my own defense..."

"John, oh John, how could you?" cried Mrs. Sloan. Mrs. Sloan was watching at her parents' house down in Valdosta, Georgia. She had invited all of her girlfriends from Valdosta High. Estelle had a lot of friends and some of them had to sit on the floor. Mrs. Sloan wanted to share her pride in her husband, but as her husband spoke there was no pride to share. Sloan's words were as shocking as a surprise fingerwave. How could he say such things? How could he? John, you bastard. The thoughts spewed out. I've always remained true. I never ever even looked at another man. A wife for sixteen years, now this. I was so proud of you. Daddy was so proud of you. How could you? I'll never be able to face my friends again. What will Daddy think? "I always said that boy was no good," said the father.

At the White House the man in the wing chair screamed, "Get that fucker off the air."

Ziegler waddled out to call the networks.

Back at Clark Field, Admiral Gayler was whispering in one of General Moore's ears. What was said has been lost to history.

Sloan continued, his pace picking up, "...many leave the field of battle under fire. Break and run. It remains for the American people, the Court-martial and the soldier himself to answer the question: is deserting in the face of the enemy any less a crime than surrendering to the enemy? Americans are lenient toward the man who runs at the first shot. Should they imprison the man who is captured, surrenders to save his life? Does not the man..."

"Ziegler, Ziegler get him off. Get him off now. This President won't stand for such talk." The President's blood pressure peaked to 190/140. The White House Press Secretary got Colonel Wellborne on the COSMIC DELTA line. It is impossible to record both ends of a COSMIC DELTA conversation, but as young Wellborne remembers, the Press Secretary said, "Get that fuck off the air."

Colonel Wellborne relayed a message to that effect to the public relations man, who relayed it to the trailer cum control booth. There, the network pool unit director, a large man by the name of Stanley Losack said, "It's too good to cut. I'm feeding."

Sloan, unaware of the trouble he was causing in high places, went on, "...deserve the same treatment as a coward. What about my actions in prison? I did not confess to anything, although many did. I did not give out the codes and frequencies, although many did. I did not steal food from my fellow prisoners, although some did. I did not squeal on my fellow prisoners, although some did. I tried to escape, although most did not. I worried about upholding a little honor, while most of the parachutists worried about who was the ranking senior officer..."

"Turn it off, I can't stand such talk," said the father. "Mother of God," said Estelle.

"Ziegler, Ziegler, call Nickleman, call the network presidents, call Cronkite, call Barbara Walters. Get him off, I say. Call the Army. He's an enemy. " The President was jumping up and down like a troll in heat.

An EGRESS RECAMP communications specialist pulled the plug to the power supply feeding the trailer. The red light on the camera went out.

Down in Pensacola, George Nickleman was watching all of this in his beach house. He was tuned to Channel 5 Mobile, Alabama.

A young woman, pretty as a sweet pea, was rubbing his private parts. Sometimes Nickleman's private part takes a lot of persuasion. The Sweet Pea is a wonderful persuader. Colonel Sloan's speech caused Mr. Nickleman's penis to lose what little erection it had. "Holy shit," said George Nickleman, "The asshole is going to blame me for this."

All in all, Operation EGRESS RECAMP assembled 2869 people of all descriptions at Clark Field. Included in this figure are of course all of the EOD officers and a substantial number of FAOs. They amassed hoards of public relations men, psychiatrists, psychologists and sign painters and medical men of all kinds: gastroenterologists, bone men, orthopedic surgeons, lower back and right leg pain men, skin men, tropical disease men and some old time TB men, urologists, neurologists, but no gynecologists. Paymasters were piled on top of bookkeepers. CID men and personnel specialists and base locater officers and mimeograph machine operators and photographers, lots of photographers and cooks.

The POWs, or the ex-POWs as they were now, were quartered in the base hospital. All were dressed in the hospital's pajamas and wore maroon and white dressing gowns. After a busy day of eating and medical examinations, most of the men were bussed to the Clark Field PX, so that they might buy some of the things they had lusted after for so long. The PX employees volunteered to stay overtime without pay and keep the PX open after hours, allowing the ex-POWs to shop in peace. Someone on the EGRESS RECAMP with the usual attention to details sent a letter to each and every one of the PX workers, signed by Richard M. Nixon.

Sloan and Kleinschmidt stayed behind. Both thought they had best husband their money for legal fees. Sloan, dressed in the hospital's PJs, sat on a chair. His feet were on the bed. He looked casual as can be. He was worried sick.

"Come in, Littlesmith, care for a drop of gin?"

"Gin, where did you get gin? "

"Son, I got it from the fellow that empties the bed pans. I've never been in a hospital yet where the bedpan emptier couldn't get you a little gin. You usually have to tip 'em, but this fellow wouldn't even let me pay for the gin. Strange guy.

"But then it is a strange calling."

Kleinschmidt didn't realize that most people have no control over their destiny. He thought if one wanted to become a lawyer and couldn't get into Harvard, one went to Yale. If one wanted to be a bedpan emptier or a garbage man or a sewer cleaner or a rag and bone man, one did just that.

"I'll have some gin. Say don't you think vodka would be a little safer?"

"Not on your life. The first thing the nurses think of is vodka, but gin fools them every time. Just fill that water thing, the carafe or whatever with gin and pitch the empty bottles down the clothes chute. That's the way the doctors do it. We patients are in the clear."

Sloan poured two large gins. Gin is sort of a non-prescription diazepam.

"What'd you think of my speech? I didn't want to talk, but they made me."

"Damn fine speech. First rate."

"Hell, what do you make of it, Littlesmith? "

"The gin, er, it's fine, best I've had in years." That's the truth.

"No, no, I mean the way they're treating us. "

"Best I can make out, Major, is that they think us some sort of heroes or something."

"Do you think we should start acting like heroes then? No, I couldn't do that. How about some more gin?"

"No thanks, I'm still working on this one."

Sloan poured himself a very large gin. "Maybe we should act like modest heroes until we find out what it is they think we've done. But, I tell you I don't like this whole thing one bit."

"We're heroes, dumb fucking heroes from a dumb fucking war. Do you think we can get away with it, I mean keep out of prison?"

"No one ever gets away with anything. We all have to pay the piper one Hay or the other."

"You're living in the 19th century, Major. There is no such thing as Justice."

Kleinschmidt is a lawyer and should know about justice, so we'll have to take his word about it.

"This is serious business, Littlesmith. I want to stay in the Army. I don't want to be drummed out. What the fuck should I do?"

"Listen, say as little as possible. Remember what you tell 'em. We'll stick to the same story if we find out what the fuck it is. Jesus, I can't think." Sloan poured another large gin.

"How can I tell them anything? I doubt they're going to ring us up. But one never knows in the Army. I think it must be a case of mistaken identity. I can imagine what sort of a story they heard about us."

"It must have been a fucking whopper· Look at the reception we're getting. Shit, John Glenn didn't have it this good."

"They are treating the parachutists pretty good too."

"That's one I can't figure out."

When the sun comes up in Washington, it goes down in the Philippines. As Mr. Nixon bangs his morning Sanka cup, Sloan sips his gin. Twelve hours later, Mr. Nixon would sip his gin and Sloan would curse the morning and drink his coffee. Neither man was a morning drinker, much to their credit.

It was nine in the morning in Washington, which makes it nine at night in the Philippines. The President asked Manolo for another cup of Sanka and called for Haldeman. Sloan poured himself another large gin, a Largos gin.

Haldeman had already gone over the day's schedule with Steve Bull. Bull, or "old full of" as he is known to some of the younger members of the White House staff, checked with the heads of the FAOs and the EODs and EGRESS RECAMP for advice and consent on the selection of the POW of the day. The trouble was that Bull was super efficient and had done all this before the POWs arrived at Clark. Mr. Pat Buchanan knew that the Pres (Mr. Buchanan called the President, the Pres) had watched Sloan's speech on the tube (Mr. Buchanan called a television set, the tube) and included no mention of Sloan's speech in the daily press summary. No murmur of Sloan's heresy was heard around the White House or the EOB for that matter. Even the boys in the pressroom didn't bring it up at Ziegler's morning briefing. Such were the totems, the sacred bulls of the time. The New York Times and

The Washington Post did not carry an account of Sloan's speech.

It was as if it never happened. Steve Bull hadn't watched Sloan on television so he had no way of knowing what happened. Bull was a hard worker and rarely looks at the tube. Haldeman forgot Sloan's name and said later, "There is room only for so much trivia."

The President didn't catch Sloan's name. Mr. Nixon wasn't too good at catching names. The name Sloan meant nothing to him.

Haldeman enters.

P- Hi Bob, sit down.

H- Good morning.

P- What's up today?

H- Same old shit.

P- The POWs are going over pretty big aren't they? You've got to hand it to old Nickleman.

H- I never dreamed it would be so good. We should have brought them home before the elections. That bastard McGovern wouldn't have carried Massachusetts or even been put on the ballot down South, if we had brought them home in October.

P- Yeah, but this President won anyway. If only this President had known. If only Kissinger had listened to Le Duc Tho, we could have got them home in time. But he kept insisting on only 1160 members of the peacekeeping force. Say, who did the sampling?

H- That dope Harris. We should have used Gallup.

P- Well--er, anyway the POWs will serve us well for the next four years; might help us out of any tight spots that might come up--not that I think any will, mind you.

H- Nothing to worry about. No hot spots, now that Pat Gray is over at FBI and Dick Helms is covering for us over at the CIA. As long as we have men like John Dean and Tony Ulasewicz on our team, no one will send us to prison.

P- Those POWs are really something else, aren't they?

H- Yeah, the POWs are like busing, only positive, only positive.

P- Yeah, positive; we need some positive issues during this President's second term.

H- Maybe we can use them for the whole time. I'll have Ziegler work out some long range PR plans. You know, maybe an honor guard made up of POWs or something.

P- Sounds good. Maybe old Nickleman has some ideas.

H- I'll try the old fart.

P- Say, do I have anything to do today?

H- You're scheduled to call a Colonel John H. Sloan, the POW of the day. He was a prisoner for six years. His wife is a big shot in the POW Wives and Families Association. He is standing by on line 5.

P- His wife is not that fat dame with the crooked wig, is she? I can't stand that dumb stupid (expletive deleted).

[Author's note: This is from the official White House Transcript.]

H- No, Bull checked that out. Ziegler is trying to keep her off the air for good. Her and that fucker Cronkite.

P- What's the guy's name again?'

H- Sloan, Colonel John H. Sloan.

P- Air Force?

H- No, Army.

P- Was he a soldier? This President didn't know there were any soldiers.

H- There weren't many, but this dope was in the infantry.

P- Fought huh?

H- I doubt it.

The President pushed the blinking button 5. "Colonel Sloan, this is the President of the United States of America, your Commander in Chief, Richard M. Nixon. The President and all good Americans are, well, frankly proud of what you done, er, did."

This was Sloan's big chance. Now he could find the cause for the mistake. The President was proud of him, and he should know, if anyone did. Soon he would have the answer to all these honors. His hand trembled slightly. His mouth was dry. He took a sip of gin and said, "Thank you, Mr. President. Why are you proud of me?"

"Er, well, we are proud of all you brave men. You will have our support as long as we live. "

"Because of what Littlesmith and I did, Mr. President?"

"Yeah, er--The President recognized Sloan's voice. Mr. Nixon made a terrible face. Mr. Nixon is not much on names, but a good ear he does have. The President made an obscene gesture right under Haldeman's nose. Haldeman got up and left the oval office.

"What was it exactly, Mr. President. I mean, what did we do to make you so proud and want to support us as long as we live? We were prisoners for six years."

"Ah, er, that's why we are proud of you. We brought you home on your feet instead of your knees, as some people would do--does--have it. I don't mean to be critical of anyone, that's not the American way."

"Mr. President, you mean to say you are proud of us just because we were prisoners?"

Haldeman was on the extension in Rose Mary Wood's office. Haldeman recognized the voice. It is unclear just what Halde-man said. The gin fogged Sloan's verbatim memory. Haldeman claims he doesn't remember having the conversation. Mr. Nixon says the conversation is protected by the principle of confi-dentiality.

The log of White House telephone calls next shows a four minute fifty-three second call to George Nickleman at Pensacola Beach. I don't know what was said. There is no way to force Mr. Nixon or old Nickleman to give the details of their conversation. All I know is that the Sweet Pea remembers the call and said of that call: "Poor Poopsie, no matter how hard I tried, Poor Poop-sie could never get it up again after that call from the President.

Hundreds of Filipino tailors stitched and sewed throughout the night so the ex-prisoners might dress in something military in the morning. The original EGRESS RECAMP plan called for tailors to be flown in from Hong Kong. But someone on Dr. Roger Shield's staff was the watchdog of the public money and specified indigenous tailors. Watchdog of the public money is a term used by bureaucrats. They use the term in jest. It is used seriously on this page. The tailors were paid $1.25 an hour including overtime. That should show how seriously the term is used.

The ex-POWs were very popular items. Everyone at Clark wanted to see them, touch them, talk to them, and even smell them. The press, the civilian contractors and the sizable military force at Clark pressed in worshipping, venerating, idolizing the former prisoners. These men were Sam Houston, Davy Crockett, General George Armstrong Custer, Sergeant York, Black Jack Pershing, Charles Augustus Lindbergh, Colin Kelly, Douglas Macarthur, Homer Young, Ira Hayes and Virgil Grissom all rolled into one grand public relations package. Each and every man, be he cook, baker, or bombardier, coward or hero was in the minds of the people: Hero.

The correspondents wanted to interview the ex-prisoners. That is why their papers and television stations sent them across twelve time zones. The EOD officers would not let the reporters interview their men. EGRESS RECAMP handed out piles of press releases to make up for the lack of interviews. Anyone can sit in a bar and copy over an EGRESS RECAMP press release.

A lot of reporters did. But a real reporter should at least try to seek the truth for himself. A few reporters did. When the heroes talked to these reporters, their EOD officers got angry. They told their wards over and over again, "Come on, you guys aren't playing the game. If you talk to civilians, you'll jeopardize the release of the prisoners still held in Vietnam." It was difficult to get an interview with one o£ the ex-prisoners.

No one said just what the ex-POWs could or would say that would possibly make the government in Hanoi keep the few sad men they still held. Even General Rex King wondered. He didn't tell a soul of his wonderings.

The doctors were astonished. They understood that the men would look like General Wainwright. They understood they would have malaria, worms and un-named tropical diseases, beriberi, paratyphoid and scurvy. The doctors thought some of them would be crazy. One psychiatric officer made this prediction: "They (the POWs) will be screwed up psychologically." In the precise language of psychiatry, screwed up psychologically means loony. The only prisoner even the least bit worried about being Looney was Little Lamar. And the only time he worried were the times he had an erection.

All of the worries were false, Little Lamar's and the psychiatric officer's included. One doctor, a man in the liver and gall bladder business, said, "Shit, if all my patients looked as good as these boys (the ex-POWs), I'd have to sell the Mercedes."

Mercedes is doctor talk for a Mercedes-Benz automobile.

It was another one of the psychiatric officer's premonitions that made a fraud of most of EGRESS RECAMP's good work. That premonition was: "When he (the POW) comes back, if you have vanilla and chocolate ice cream, don't ask him which he wants, just give him one, because he won't be able to make decisions." The ex-POWs are all professional military men and had lasted all those years in the service and for months if not years in a prison camp and they knew full well what kind of ice cream they wanted, if indeed they wanted ice cream at all. After all those years in prison, the men, when served vanilla ice cream when they did not ask for it, would more than likely say, "For Christ sake, don't you have any gin?"

One of the wives: a nice lady from California, who knew a good deal more about things than the psychiatric officer said, "My husband is no goddamn baby."

EGRESS RECAMP realized the prisoners were, as Dr. Roger Shields himself said, "In A-OK condition." "A-OK" is an expression used by astronauts meaning good or very good. The ex-POWs not only stole the astronaut's place in the hearts of Americans, they took their language as well.

"Why waste time? Let us send home the prisoners," said Dr. Roger Shields. I don't know what kind of doctor Doctor Shields is. He could be a dentist, but I doubt it. I don't think he is a gall bladder man, but he could be. I bet he is one of those Doctor Kissinger kind of doctors. Whatever kind he is, he is a very fine man.

America was screaming for POWs. Everybody wanted the POWs to come to their towns. The political pressure on the Pentagon was intense. General Haig ordered the POWs to be flown home in small batches, with each batch landing in a different city. General Haig believes in sharing the wealth, not that he is a communist mind you. Three planes landed in various cities in California and one in Honolulu. The POWs were very popular down south and in Texas and he sent a few planeloads there. General Haig stretched the POWs out the best he could. The POWs were on their way home. They were very happy.

Regina King was about as randy as a person can get. People sometimes get very randy. A teenager in the first flush of love would be no match for Mrs. King. How she ached. She throbbed. She longed for someone to cuddle her, cuddle her and whisper baby talk in her ear, nibble at her ear and speak nonsense. Someone to gently rub the insides of her thighs and hold her tight. The wet finger slowly circling her nipple, that the nipple would stand erect. The soft caress of the lips of her vagina. What pleasure. The touch, the kiss. Oh, God, Mrs. King could hardly stand it. Mrs. King's bed, empty for six years, was empty now. Not that it had been all that full before that. Just as Mrs. King had lost pounds and pounds in Rex King's mind, Colonel King, now General King had become more tender and loving in Mrs. King's mind. Gin is a substitute, but it can't take place of someone to hold you tight on a winter's night.

After the interview with Walter Cronkite, Regina thought she couldn't stand being away from Rex for even twenty-four more hours. The network booked her a deluxe room in a Washington Hilton. A Washington Hilton is called for some reason the Statler Hilton. It is the exception that proves the rule. The rule, of course, is: Hilton hotels take the names of cities. Statler is not another name for Washington.

Regina drank on her gin and quinine water. She was naked and smoked a filter tip menthol cigarette. The room smelled ever so bad. It was a deluxe room and deluxe rooms have mirror-covered dressing rooms. She held her hand up under her huge left breast so that the nipple rested between her thumb and forefinger. Finer, prettier nipples could not be found. Surely they were the finest nipples ever. She had skin to match. The skin was fine, transparent and clear--luminous, clear and smooth as a baby's bottom. Mrs. King moved her left hand in a slow clockwise direction, squeezing what she could of her giant breast and slightly pinching its nipple. Mrs. King moaned out loud, "Rex, oh Rex." An ash fell from the menthol filter tip cigarette.

Mrs. King picked up the dial telephone (deluxe rooms have telephones in the dressing rooms) and dialed "0." The telephone had a template with oversized Arabic numbers and small printing. The small print said: "room service, abc, valet, def, pool, ghi, local, lks, long distance, mno, front desk, prs, garage, tuv, 164 bell captain, wxy and operator." Mrs. King dialed the operator.

The operator, good person that it is, answered.

"Get me Father McNaughton at the White House," Mrs. King said,

"Yes, right away, Mrs. King," answered the operator. Mrs. King was an important guest at the Hilton and the Hilton, as I say, gives good service. You should try their dry martinis and see how clean their bathrooms are. Never mind that it is called the Statler Hilton. Make believe it is the Washington Hilton. Mrs. King was put right through to Father McNaughton, S.J.

Father McNaughton answered and said, "Frank McNaughton, hello."

"Father McNaughton, this is Regina King."

"Oh yes, Mrs. King, I was just thinking about you and was go into call you." That is true. Father McNaughton had received his American Express bill and was going to call her about the ticket on Southern Airways.

"Could you find out Rex's port of arrival for me?" Each group of prisoners was to land at different cities. These cities were called ports of arrival.

"Port of what?"

"Port of arrival, you know, where Rex is going to land. I want to meet him."

"Hawaii, I think." General King was quite the most popular POW at the Whit e House after his speech at Clark. Every one around the White House knew all about him. They all knew little tidbits of information about him. Everyone knew what he had for breakfast and things like that. Everyone loved Rex King. Nixon loved Rex King; Old George Nickleman told Richard Nixon, "Shit,

I thought him up."

"Can't you find out for sure? I'm going to meet him."

"Sure, I'll put you on hold. Just wait one second, Mrs. King."

He put her on hold. The hold button at the White House plays music while you are being held. The White House is very up to date. Father McNaughton called Dr. Roger Shields. Sure enough, Rex King was coming in to Honolulu at five the next afternoon.

"Honolulu, here I come. I'm on my way, buster. " Mrs. King hung up with those words.

Regina King took a United Airlines 747 direct to the Hawaiian Island. The friendly skies were ever so friendly. The stewardess averted her eyes as Regina King rubbed the insides of her thighs.

Sloan's hometown of record is Valdosta, Georgia. Valdosta bears no resemblance to its namesake Valle d'Aosta. Sloan had spent little time in Valdosta over the past twenty-two years. He hadn't even been there since his mother died some ten or so years ago. Estelle went home every summer to visit her folks, leaving Sloan to fix his own breakfasts. Sloan joined the Army more to get out of Valdosta than to get into the Army. He hated the town. His boyhood friends were gone; killed in logging accidents or by booze or in the Navy--a lot of Valdosta boys join the Navy. Most of his childhood friends had merely changed beyond all recognition. Gone, too, was the Pure Oil Station where Sloan wasted so much of his youth drinking Nehi

Oranges or Royal Crown Colas half full of peanuts, or bottles of Squirt half full of gin or pitching pennies or "baiting niggers." The Pure Oil Station on North Ashley Street was gone and so was Sloan's youth.

The people of Valdosta heard Sloan's speech at Clark, but cast his words aside. Only Estelle Sloan and the father took the words to heart. Sloan was a POW and he was from Valdosta and the Valdostonians loved him. Sloan was known as Valdosta's own.

February 18, 1973, was declared John H. Sloan Day in the Turpentine Capitol of the world. EGRESS RECAMP headed Sloan directly toward Lowndes County. The citizenry labored hard at having Sloan come directly from Travis Air Force Base to Valdosta. A committee, chaired by a person named Big Bob Haggerty, hired a behind-the- scenes politico lawyer for that end. The lawyer, a greasy man, oiled the way. It was said that he contacted Bo Callaway, Her-man Talmadge and Sam Nunn and Roy Ginn, Dawson Mathis, Jack Brinkley, Ben Blackburn, Johnny Flint, Billy Stuckey, Phil Lan-drum and Bobbie Stevens. I don't know if that is true or not. I do know the lawyer said, "I didn't bother with that nigger, Andy Young." Whatever he did, it worked. Colonel John H. Sloan came directly from his port of entry to Valdosta. General Haig was glad to have Sloan in an obscure part of the nation.

One thing else worthy of note in Sloan's quick dispatch to Valdosta: EGRESS RECAMP had been ordered by General Haig not to let Colonel Sloan say one word, not one single word in public. More than one public relations officer came on the jet with Sloan to make sure General Haig's wish was carried out. Big Bob Hag-gerty and the greasy lawyer were made to take an oath that Sloan would not talk in public. The oath was the main reason that General Haig and EGRESS RECAMP let Sloan come to Valdosta in such a rush.

In Valdosta, Sloan found his mail waiting for him. Sacks and sacks of mail, tons of mail, mailed by people unknown. There were afghan rugs crocheted by little old ladies over many a gin on long winter's nights. There were ecology posters, shaving lotion--enough shaving lotion to float the Coast Guard---and oddly, hundreds, no, thousands and thousands of pictures and posters and images of a sea gull. Strange.

Stranger still were the hundreds of pounds of John H. Sloan bracelets. Tens of thousands of people mailed their John H. Sloan bracelets to Valdosta, Georgia. Newspapers all over the land published the addresses of the returning prisoners and millions of citizens took it into their heads to mail their bracelets back to the bracelet's namesake. Why we do not know.

Hundreds of postmen were cut by the improperly wrapped bracelets.

The automatic equipment ordered by Red Blount from Pitney-Bowes and IT&T did not take into account the possibility of people mailing cupro-nickel bracelets in plain white envelopes. The machines bent, ripped and mangled the bracelets. The bracelets took their revenge by jamming the expensive machines and cruelly cutting the postmen's hands. The machinery required extensive repairs and the postmen had to get tetanus shots.

Thousands and thousands of Valdostonians and a few of the timber millionaires and doctors came to Valdosta International Airport. Billy Cobb came along with his new wife. The timber millionaire's daughter was just a memory now. Estelle Sloan and the father did not come. "There's no telling what that boy will say. I will not be disgraced in my own town. I will not go to the airport," said the father.

"And neither will I," said Estelle Sloan. She didn't want to face Sloan. After his statement at Clark, Estelle retched every time she thought of Sloan coming home and trying to make love to her. The idea of him putting his hard penis inside her caused her to vomit for hours.

The American Legion was out at Valdosta International Airport along with their crack drum and bugle corp. Both the Amvets and the Veterans of Foreign Wars provided honor guards. The

Hadji Temple presented their precision motorcycle stunt teams. The high schools of the surrounding counties of Echols, Lanier, Berrien, Cook and Brook sent their bands and majorettes. The Shrine Oriental band provided welcome relief from the Moody Air

Force marching band. The officers of the Elks, Rotary, Lions, Kiwanis, Civitans, Toastmasters, Optimists, Chamber of Commerce and the Jaycees were all there. The Worshipful Masters of the many Masonic Lodges Here there along with the Commander of the Malta Commanders and the Governor of the Mooses and the Post commander of the Jewish War Veterans and the High Priest of the Royal Arch and the Mother Advisor of the Rainbow Girls. Miss Peach Blossom was there together with Miss Boll Weevil from Enterprise, Alabama, clean over in the next state. Of all the people at the Valdosta International Airport that day there was not one black, not one single one.

Big Bob provided the speakers' platform. The speakers' platform was a large Chevrolet stake truck without the stakes.

Big Bob owns Haggerty's Chevrolet, located in car city on the Indianola Road.

"Bob Haggerty and his men of integrity," reads the motto of Haggerty's Chevrolet. Big Bob still goes on test-drives with his old customers. He is not above taking a wrench in hand when one of his Chevrolets comes back for warrant re-pairs. Big Bob sells one heck of a lot of Chevrolets. It is said that he gives good trade-ins. The men of integrity sell many a Chevy by saying; "Big Bob will disconnect all those buzzers and all that pollution stuff at no extra charge if you will take the appearance package." The appearance package makes a Chevrolet look just awful. It is a very popular extra.

McNeil's Funeral Home wanted the dignitaries to have some place to sit, so they sent a bunch of folding chairs. The Holiday Inn out on Highway 94 (the new Statenville Road) wanted a little free advertising, so they sent the podium. On the front of the podium are the words Holiday Inn printed in their distinctive logotype and color. Their color is green. If you have ever faced the morning in a Holiday Inn, you will know the reason for that color. The cream-colored fire engines from the Valdosta Volunteer Fire Department were polished and shiny and there. So too was a sizable contingent of orange and blue Georgia State Patrol cars. The cars were all Chevrolets. The Blue Angels, the Navy acrobatic flyers, flew overhead and did their acrobatics. It was rumored that Lieutenant Governor Lester "Axe Handle" Maddox was there, but no one I talked to actually saw him. The Army Sky Divers were there and everybody saw them dive. Governor Carter was there, smiling for all to see. He sat on one of McNeil's folding chairs.

Sylvester J. McNeil later put a small brass plaque on that chair saying: Jimmy Carter sat in this chair on February 18, 1973. Still later someone put a piece of chewing gum over the word "sat" and wrote in blue ballpoint ink above the chewing gum: rested his ass.

The main event, the real attraction, was Sloan himself.

There have never been many heroes from Valdosta, but now they had one or at least they thought they had one--and they were proud. As Big Bob said as he stood behind the Holiday Inn podium, "By golly we're proud. We're button busting proud of Valdosta's own John E. Sloan."

"H," said Sloan, correcting Big Bob.

That was the only thing Sloan said in public that day. General Haig would have been pissed by even that one letter. General Haig is a real stickler for rules. The letter of the law as he would say. It is a good thing he didn't find out about that letter. I do hope I am not violating any confidences by recording the letter H on this page.

Colonel Sloan sat on one of McNeil's folding chairs. Governor Carter sat to his right. Governor Carter looked at Sloan from time to time and smiled. Governor Carter smiles a lot and is long of tooth. Sloan wasn't smiling. He looked out at the crowd trying to spot Estelle. Surely she would come to the air-port to meet him. He longed so to see her, hold her and make love. In the six years of prison fantasies, Sloan was sure that Estelle could enjoy sex if only he could get it right. Sloan had devised several methods to ensure Estelle's pleasure. Where was she? He needed to talk to her. She would understand. She could advise him what to do. Was he a fool or a hero? A coward or a hypocrite?

He was really just a soldier trying to get by. Now he was caught in a swamp of lies. Estelle would understand. He would tell her the whole story. Where was she?

Sloan looked out over the crowd. The crowd was hysterical with pride and joy. The good folk of South Georgia were out-doing the folks at Clark in their adoration of a single POW. The people in the Eastern Time Zone were just as confused as the people on Central Philippine Time. That confusion was between the then President Nixon and the former prisoners. The Presi-dent and the former prisoners seemed interchangeable in the crowd's mind. What was praise for one was praise for the other. The confusion was not total, however. While there were plenty of signs saying, "Welcome Home Sloan," there were no signs saying, "God Loves Sloan." There were plenty of signs calling down God's blessings and acknowledging His love for one Richard Nixon and handsome signs they were too. The signs welcoming Sloan and acknowledging his place of birth looked homemade and had a certain naïveté to them. One of the timber millionaires called the signs charming.

The crowd could barely be contained. The throng had gone into an ecstasy, blissless exaltation, when Sloan stepped off the Air Force Jetstar II (Where are you Mr. Houghton?). The Georgia State Patrol was tried as it held back the multitude. Barely pubescent girls were outflanked by DAR ladies in full battle dress, mink stoles, sashes, medals and orchid corsages, in their quest to lay finger on a real live, living, breathing POW. An American Legion Queen Anne drill team from a forgotten town in Georgia was pressed into service to hold back the sweating Rotarians and all those United Daughters of the Confederacy in their half size dresses.

Sloan smiled for the first time when he realized he didn't have to make another statement in front of the television cameras. He had eyed with fear the television cameras from Atlanta. It was only his thoughts of Estelle that kept fear in tow.

Finally the rally was over. And was Sloan ever glad to get into the Chevrolet convertible and be driven off. The Chevrolet was driven by one of the men of integrity. The parade took him into the heart of downtown Valdosta, a mean and miserable place. The odd colored fire engines with red lights flashing, the sleek cruiser cars of the Georgia State Patrol with blue lights turning, the motorcycles' roar with their bitter sirens wailing from time to time, the bands, the flashing legs of the majorettes and the wide view of their crotches should have added to the merriment of the day.

Sloan was made to ride in the back seat of Big Bob's con-vertible. He looked uncomfortable and undemocratic. A guest of honor riding in the back seat of a convertible is supposed to wave, so Sloan waved for a while. He asked the man of integrity to drop him off on Calhoun Drive after the parade. The man of integrity didn't answer. He looked like a bishop caught in a lie.

News travels fast in Valdosta.

The joyous crowds were left behind at the International Airport. The few that could make it to their cars joined in the parade and honked their horns madly. There are never many people in downtown Valdosta, only the poor, the black and the people without cars and only a few of those. Valdosta is well supplied with poor and blacks and people without cars. That crowds one finds in Valdosta are at the new shopping center out on the new Statenville Road or at the big game between the Valdosta High School VIPs (Valdosta's Important Players) and the Thomasville Tigers or at the Valdosta International Airport when a POW returns. The crowds are not found downtown. Indeed a number of the timber millionaires liked to brag that they hadn't been downtown in twenty years. Most of the doctors could say honestly, "I've never been downtown. " What people there were in town watched the passing parade in silence. A few waved, all looked embarrassed and none looked Sloan in the eye. Their eyes seemed focused on the slowly turning tires of Big Bob's Chevrolet.

Sloan stopped waving.

Having lots of money is dangerous to your mind. First off, one can buy lots of things with lots of money. That occupies the mind and leads to boring conversation. Second off, the rich come to think they deserve to be rich. If you don't think that leads to boring conversation, try talking to a gynecologist about tax shelters. Third off, the rich become intensely patriotic.

If you really want to be bored, ask a Texas oil man what he thinks of the First Amendment (explain it to him first). If you can't find a Texas oil man or a gynecologist there are plenty of lawyers around. Not all lawyers make lots of money, but most do. It is quite the best way to make lots of money without getting ones hands dirty in the literal sense. Karen Schuster's firm makes pots and pots of money by dirtying their hands in the metaphorical sense. They, of course, think they deserve all that money. They buy lots of things. The partners are subject to acute attacks of patriotism. The worst attack of patriotism I have ever seen was the one the Ambassador (the senior partner) had when he realized that Karen's boyfriend was not only a POW, but a Yale lawyer as well. Well, the senior partner went into a patriotic frenzy. It was terrible and frightening. It went on for quite some time (patriotic frenzies are difficult to time with any precision). There was talk of calling a doctor. Finally the Ambassador recovered and stammered, "We have got to have your young man in the firm. Just imagine, just imagine a POW with Scarf, Swineshit and Bog." The Ambassador gave Karen the month off to meet, fuck and recruit Justin Kleinschmidt.

Kleinschmidt arrived before the patriotic frenzy, so Karen couldn't meet him when he arrived. The Ambassador called old George Nickleman, who called the POW Locator Service (POWLS). Kleinschmidt was in San Francisco staying at the Fairmount Hotel. POWLS didn't report that Kleinschmidt was staying with one of the Marilyn Chamberses, but he was. In fact, at the very moment of the Ambassador's attack Justin Kleinschmidt was fucking the nurse, dog style.

To San Francisco went Karen Schuster. She tried calling Kleinschmidt's room, but Kleinschmidt didn't answer nor did the Marilyn Chambers. They were performing an act that is illegal in California even between consenting adults. There was nothing to do but wait around and wait she did. By now she actually thought she was in love with Justin. If she trusted her memory, she would still be hurt and angry with him. Kleinschmidt had treated her shamefully in New Haven.

The Fairmount has a splendid swimming pool sunken in a wide terrace. Karen was waiting on that terrace. She was drinking a kir while she waited. And thinking of Justin while she was drinking, and while thinking of Justin, she saw Justin in person come out for a swim. After what Kleinschmidt and the nurse had been doing, I hope he took a shower before his swim. The nurse stayed in the room. She was too sore to swim.

Justin dove in and swam a few quick laps. Then he spotted Karen's tits. They looked vaguely familiar. Karen's face stirred no memories. Kleinschmidt had run out of things to do with and to the nurse. Big tits would be a nice change, Kleinschmidt thought. What the hell, I'll give it a try. He went up to Karen and said, "Don't I know you from somewhere?"

"Justin, darling, it's me."

"Don't tell me. I know you. We met at Bunny Arbuckle's that summer. You know when you and all those other crazy girls rented that house in Cutchogue. "

"Justin, it's me, Karen Schuster."

"Karen, I'll be goddamned." He remembered the nipples.

"Oh Justin, darling. " Karen hugged Justin and pressed her tits close to Justin's wet body.

"Have you a room here? "

"Yes, why? "

"You'll find out."

And she did.

The next day Kleinschmidt went back to the Marilyn Chambers' room and said, "I've just come to get my luggage honey."

Kleinschmidt took the job at Scarf, Swineshit and Bog. He started at 175,000 a year in their Wills and Estates Department. I don't know much about the law, but it seems to me that one would have to cheat many a widow and orphan to earn 175,000 a year.

By the time Regina King arrived at the Honolulu International Airport, she was a little calmer. A middle-aged lady can only stay in heat for so long. Then, too, she drank more than a few gins in the friendly skies. She received grand treatment at the airport. They gave her orchid lei. A lei is not a lay. A lei is a necklace of flowers. Her luggage was collected for her and a limousine provided by the local chapter of the Association of the POW Wives and Families. She told the driver, "Take me to the Honolulu Hilton."

"Sorry Missy, but there's no such place."

The driver was a Filipino. He knew Oahu the way he knew how to talk to American ladies.

"What kind of a fucking town is this?"

"Oh, I bet Missy means Hilton Hawaiian Village."

"As long as they have clean bathrooms, I guess it will do."

"Oh yes Missy, very clean."

Mrs. King booked the bridal suite. She had been planning this day for six years. It had come at last. She went to her suite to unpack, douche and take a hot bath. She had bought a number of things just for this one day. The most expensive item was the new Pucci dress. I frankly didn't know that Mr. Pucci made dresses that large. If one didn't know better, one would think Mr. Pucci a tent maker. She had a new wig made of Spanish nun's hair. She had a new bottle of Joy. And just· three days ago she had bought a new product called Vagilube. She doubted she would need it, but with Rex you never know. She had a new Frederick's of Hollywood nightgown. The gown went by the trade name of peek-nique. And for Rex she had bought an ointment called Staylong. The motto for this product is: Last long with Staylong.

Mrs. King called room service and ordered a bottle of Piper-Heidsieck on the off chance that Rex had given up Christ and taken up booze in prison. She also ordered a large gin and quinine water for drinking in the tub.

The crowds were gathering when Mrs. King rode back to the airport. It was only 3:00p.m. But the place was getting crowded. With hours to kill, Mrs. King made her way to the airport bar. There is a proper drink to drink in most airport bars. In Athens it is ouzo. In Rome it is Campari and soda. At Heathrow it is a pint of bitters. At Haneda it is sake. In Malaga it is Tio Pepe. At the Honolulu International Airport it is gin and pineapple juice. Mrs. King ordered and drank gin and pineapple juices whilst she waited. Her libido picked up with each passing minute. She calmed herself with gin and pineapple juice.

By 4:00 p.m. the crowds were enormous. CINCPAC (you'll recall my telling you to remember this) was there along with many an aide. Mrs. CINCPAC stayed home in the lovely house provided by the American taxpayers for whoever happened to be CINCPAC. The Gaylers were planning the biggest t party of the season in honor of Rex King. Mrs. Gayler wasn't taking any chances of something going wrong.

"Noel will take care of things at the airport," said Mrs. CINCPAC.

As the clock moved toward five, Mrs. King moved through the crowd. Viewed from a certain angle, Mrs. King was a little pretty in her own way. Most horny women have a certain appeal. Mrs. King is no exception. Mrs. King was still shoving her way into the crowd when Rex's plane landed.

"Out of my way. Step aside. I'm meeting my man. Out of the way, buster," roared Mrs. King.

Her orchid lei was crushed as she bore into the masses of people. Her new wig was knocked askew. The poor Spanish nun would never have recognized her own hair.

General Rex King stepped off the plane and held up his GOD BLESS NIXON! sign for all to see. Colonel Roderick Vincent Wellborne III was the first to shake his hand. Colonel Wellborne wears the gold aiguillettes of a Presidential aide. Admiral Noel A. N. Gayler made a rude comment to Wellborne and Wellborne stepped aside. CINCPAC shook General King 's hand and said, "Aloha." Aloha means hello and goodbye in the Hawaiian language. It is a very useful word to remember if you are ever in Hawaii. When CINCPAC used the word he meant hello. General King then made his usual God Bless Nixon speech. Admiral Gayler told him about the grand party. Both Rex King and Noel A. N. Gayler were weary of crowds and made their way to Admiral Gayler's limousine.

The crowd closed in trying to say aloha to General King. Some wanted to shake his hand or just touch him. King doesn't like for people to touch him. King pushed them away. Mrs. King finally rammed her way to Rex and wrapped her arms around his neck and pressed her huge bosoms close and sobbed, "Rex, oh Rex, it's so good to see you."

Rex didn't know what she was talking about and said, "Excuse me, Madame." He shook his head in bewilderment as he got into CINCPAC's Cadillac. He said to Admiral Gayler as they drove off, "Wow, these Hawaiian women are really fat." He thought the Pucci was a muumuu.

Regina King watched Rex drive off. Then she realized the truth. Rex did not recognize her

Little Lamar's port of entry was Dallas, Texas. The C-141 landed at Love Field around three in the afternoon. The crowd had been building for hours and what a crowd it was. You have never seen so many shouting, screaming, yelling, smelling, yelping, patriotic Texans at one time in your whole life. It was worse than a Super Bowl game (a Super Bowl game is a football match much favored by Texans). There were six POWs on the C-141 and sixty bands to greet them. Only the grossest estimate can be made of the size of the crowd. Captain Fritz gave his gross estimate as 195,683. He couldn't remember whether that included children under twelve or not. It was a big crowd. Why, you could fill Yankee Stadium with just the people wearing cowboy bats and boots. The official capacity of Yankee Stadium is 81,841 and that is a lot of cowboy hats no matter how you count them. The only easy thing to count at Love Field that day was the six Air Force Jetstar IIs. There was one for each POW. A private Jetstar II to take each man from his port of entry to his hometown of record.

Little Lamar got lost in the crowd. He held tightly to his DD-201 file, his REPAK file and leave papers. He had tucked his money in his shoes and was having difficulty walking. He didn't know about the Jetstar II trip. He didn't even know that there was such a thing as a Jetstar II. He hobbled to the taxi stand and asked, "How much to take me to the Greyhound Bus Station?"

"You a POW buddy?"

"Used to be. "

"Hop in. It's off the meter. Fuck the boss. "

When Little Lamar got to the Greyhound Bus Station he was just another 1188. He had to take off one of his shoes to get the 59.00 the bus company charges to ride one of their buses between Dallas and Valdosta. Little Lamar tried to hide the act of taking off his shoe. He turned his face to the wall and did a little skip on one foot. A drunk might have thought him an olive drab wounded flamingo, lost and down on its luck.

Thirty-six hours later, Little Lamar limped up to the Butte homestead. The bus passes within a mile of the farm. The driver let him out and Little Lamar walked the last mile the best he could. "Hey, Ma, it's me."

"Ain't you a sight? The Army sure ruined your feet. "

"Here Ma, this is for you." Little Lamar bought a bronze horse with an electric clock in its stomach at the bus station in New Orleans. He carried it on his lap the whole way from New Orleans. The clock played the "Anvil Chorus" on the hour and coo-cooed on the half hour. A simple chime sounded the quarter hour. The face of the clock constantly changed colors, from red to green to yellow to blue to purple and back to red again. When the horse's tail was pulled a cigarette lighter popped out of the horse's head.

"Why thank you, Little Lamar. Now get those shoes off, while I mix us up a mess of biscuits. You must be hungry."

The man of integrity dropped Sloan off at the large white frame house on Calhoun Drive. The man of integrity didn't want to but he did. The curtains parted, then closed. He heard the front door shut as he cut across the front lawn. He rang the bell. "Estelle honey, it's me, John. I'm home."

"Go away."

"Estelle it's me, John. I'm home. Let me in so I can give you a great big hug. "

"How dare you, after what you've done to me."

"Honey, people sometimes gets captured in war. I got captured. I'm sorry, but I'll make it up to you, just you wait and see. "

"You don't understand do you? You never do. "

"I couldn't help getting captured."

"That's not what I'm talking about."

"What then?" Surely she couldn't have heard about the Danang whore.

"I'd get out of here if I was you, boy."

It was the father.

"I never want to see you again," said Estelle Sloan. "We were so proud of you and then you go and ruin it. You've ruined my life. How could you? "

"Get boy. "

The father was used to talking to field hands.

"I'll be at the Holiday Inn out on the new Statenville Road. "

John H. Sloan walked back to town and bought a quart of Gordon's gin. He kept repeating over and over again, "What have I done, what have I done?"

The gloomy feeling around the executive office of the Association of POW Wives and Families grew as the work shrunk. As soon as it looked like the prisoners were coming home, Dick Westcott started cutting and pruning the workers. The days rolled by, the prisoners were home and Dick Westcott couldn't get another sweet deal going. The harder he tried the more he pruned. By the time the first men landed at Clark the office was down to the absolutely essential accountants, bookkeepers, clerks, artists, graphic designers, lino machine operators, PBX girls, typists, secretaries, printers, telephone solicitors and the very smallest cadre of public relations men and speech writers and a single combination office boy and statistician.

Dick Westcott was drinking more than usual, which means he was drinking quite a bit. The sole new idea was the pasting of paper stickers on the POW bracelets--red for missing, yellow for accounted for and green for released. It was a dumb idea. No one wanted to pay for dinky stickers. The stickers came off if the bracelet wearer sweated. Most bracelet wearers sweated in the course of their daily work. Even Rubin Askew sweats from time to time. His sticker came off.

Old George Nickleman pushed Dick Westcott into the MIA (missing in action) business. Westcott didn't like the MIA business one bit. Still, the MIA, ONLY HANOI KNOWS bumper stickers covered the office expenses. There was little left to skim. Such a pity, because most people sent cash and cash is easy to skim. Dick Westcott always said, "It's hard to skim a check. "

The reason Dick Westcott didn't fire up a classy HIA campaign was simple. He had explained to Old George Nickleman time after time, " It costs one hell of a lob of money to get a sweet deal going on something like the MIAs. And with my luck they would find the bastards. Then we'd be swinging. I couldn't even sell Welcome Home MIA stickers. Because once they find the fucks they'd be POWs. A lot of cheap sons-of-bitches would just leave their old Welcome Home POW stickers sticking to their bumpers. There is no future in the MIAs."

"They won't find them, but can you think of anything, better? "

"There is a pretty good famine shaping up in the Sahel, you know, Chad, Niger and the Sudan."

"I thought you said we waited too long. You know in my business, I'd rather have a good famine any day. Besides, I want to stop doing anything the asshole has any interest in."

"They won't believe me, Dick. " Old Nickleman knew from where he spoke. The whole missing in action business started as compassion and ended as a cruel hoax. The first men listed as missing in action were known to all but their wives to be dead beyond all doubt. Most of the wives lived in Air Force housing in some small place like Kansas. If the flyers were declared dead, their pay would stop. The wives would have to make do on 2 cents on the dollar. They would be evicted from the base housing. If the men were listed as missing all would go on just as before. What was the harm, the war would be over soon. The war continued year after bloody year and the practice of listing dead men as missing became standard operating procedure, as they say in the war business. In 1969, when the flyers started disappearing over Cambodia, they were listed as missing to hide the fact they died in Cambodia. The wives continued to receive full pay. So what's the harm?

All of the wives lost their youth. A few lost their minds.

"Haig or whatever your name is, we've got to do something about all these calls."

"What calls are those, Mr. President?" Haig was playing dumb. Obscene telephone calls started coming in earnest right after Haldeman, Ehrlichman and Dean Here fired. The President was now plagued with obscene calls. Haig wasn't sure whether the President enjoyed the calls or not. Some of the callers offered some rather practical suggestions.

"We did wait too long. I hate to think of all the time we pissed away on those goddamn POWs. He missed out on a really good famine. Shit, Khartoum looks like Dachau. If it doesn't rain soon it will be the biggest goddamn famine ever. Fucking people are starving to death for thousands of miles in all directions."

"Is anyone working it?"

"Yeah, the fucking UN of all people and those German Catholics, Caritas."

"Those krauts know a sweet deal when they see one. They are pretty damn good at raising a buck or, er, a mark," laughed old George Nickleman.

"The best in Europe or at least on the continent. They are not as good as Oxfam, of course. Fuckers, I can't understand how they can make a full time business out of famines. Leave it to the English ladies." Dick Westcott knows the business.

"Any chance of getting in on the Sahara?"

"You know how much it costs to get a sweet deal going. We've waited too long. The networks would charge us an arm and a leg for a famine special. Shit, famines are the last thing the networks want. Just think how it would look with all those starving people sandwiched between the Shake and Bake ads. The fucking networks know where they get the gravy. It wouldn't make a dime. Don't forget those fucking starving people. We have to send them something. The famine is that bad."

"Forget it then. Let's so big with the MIAs."

"Look, I've told you a hundred times, suppose they find the fucks. Then what? "

"I never got obscene calls when Haldeman had your job." Mr. Nixon did so. He didn't get all that many, but he did get them.

"Haldeman was a fine civil servant, Mr. President."

"Best I've ever known."

"That's a fact, Mr. President."

"Hell, I want you to come up with a plan. Write this President a memo on the subject. Do you have any ideas, General or what ever you are?" Mr. Nixon could never remember an aide's rank. He pondered the idea of making all of his aides into generals. That should make it easier to communicate thought the President. Somewhere, Mr. Nixon had read that ease of communication was a good thing.

"It must be someone who knows White House procedures, Mr. President." General Haig has a keen, incisive mind. Although you would have to be a dummy to think you could call 456-1414 (dial 202 first if you are a dummy calling from outside

Washington, D. C.) and have the President answer. I can guarantee in May of 1973, President Richard M. Nixon would not answer the White House switchboard. My guarantees are at least as good as the real Rolex Oyster Company's.

The President had quite a few private telephone numbers. Mr. Nixon worried about security and eavesdropping. He also liked to reward his staff and friends and political contributors with one of his private telephone numbers. You would have had to live in Washington and been at the vortex of power to know just how coveted the President's private telephone number was. Why, a cabinet official would rather walk to work, than have it known he didn't have Mr. Nixon's private number. There were fifteen private numbers in all. This made it difficult for Alexander Butterfield, and of course, for the obscene callers. The perverts wasted many a dime trying to reach the President at one of his many private numbers. There was a private number for the Lincoln bedroom, another for the family sitting room and another for the oval office and so forth. Different people were given different private numbers. Senator Howard H. Baker, Jr., for example, had the number for the family sun porch. John B. Connally could only reach the President when the President was moving his bowels.

Hugh Hefner could ring up (call) the President right in the oval office. Those were the good old days. Now when the telephone rang in the President's private toilet, the President could never be sure if it was John Connally wanting to talk about the wholesome subject of milk prices or some pervert offering some loathsome service.

"Well, Alexander," said the President. Sometimes the President's memory is quite good.

The General Haig blushed with pride upon hearing the President of the United States of America call him by his Christian name. Haig always doubted that Mr. Nixon knew his surname.

"Well as I see it, Mr. President, the problem is twofold. One, we must change the procedures and two, we must find the caller and punish him."

"It has just gotta be someone who hates me. Who could that be? One of the Kennedys?"

"None of the Kennedys have any of your private numbers, Mr. President. The caller seems to have them all. I don't want to point any fingers, Mr. President, but you have fired a lot of people lately."

"You don't think it could be that fellow Gray, do you?"

"I don't think so, Mr. President. I understand he burned all the telephone numbers along with the Christmas trash. Do you think it could be John Dean? I never trusted him."

"That weasel. He could do it, but Henry Petersen is following his every move." Henry E. Petersen was the Assistant Attorney General of the United States of America. On April 19, 1973, Henry E. Petersen was put in charge of the Watergate Investigation. The Watergate Investigation was looking into charges of the President's misconduct. John Dean was telling Henry E. Petersen everything he knew about the President's misconduct. Henry E. Petersen repeated everything John Dean said to the President. He did the repeating right in the oval office.

He didn't say one single word about obscene phone calls.

"At this point in time, Mr. President, the only thing to do is refrain from answering any of your private telephones. Just answer the COSMIC DELTA line." 'At this point in time' is a complicated way of saying now. General Haig's use of the word refrain has nothing to do with music. He used the word the way third grade teacher would when trying to get small boys to stop throwing erasers. Obscene calls never came over the COSMIC DELTA line--bad news sometimes, but never obscene calls. Mr. Nixon liked to answer the COSMIC DELTA line in the hope that it would be an international emergency. Mr. Nixon just loved international emergencies.

"Good point, er, whatever your name is. That way the President can focus on international emergencies." The President liked to focus on things. He is not a camera.

"Right, Mr. President. I'll have the telephone company divert all calls from your private numbers."

The telephone company has a department called the Obscene Telephone Calls Department. The Obscene Telephone Calls Department put a recorded message on each of the President's private phones.

The first person to call after the telephone company fixed the President's private telephones was Hugh Hefner. The record playing machine answered the oval office phone and said, "I'm sorry, but the number you have reached is no longer in active service. This is a recording." The machine seemed to imply that the oval office phone was on the retired list.

Hugh Hefner wanted to talk with the President in the worst sort of way. Mr. Hefner wanted to cadge an invitation to the POW Ball for a young woman with the very odd name of Miss February. There was nothing else for poor Mr. Hefner to do, but dial 202-456-1414 on the off chance the President might answer. "White House, good afternoon."

Those words were spoken by a White House switchboard operator. She asked that I not use her name.

"This is Hugh Hefner, I want to speak with the President of the United States of America."

"Just a minute please." The switchboard operator put Mr. Hefner on hold. Hefner heard the melody of "Tea for Two." The operator dialed Haig and said, "General Haig it's another one of those obscene callers."

Haig had nothing else to do and said, "Put him on." Then in his most general like voice, a deep baritone voice, said, "This is the President's office."

"Hell you ain't the President. I'm Hugh Hefner and I want to talk to the President, not some dipshit."

"You pervert, stop calling the President," shouted General Haig. Then he added, "Say this is not Richard Helms is it?"

"Don't call me a pervert, you cocksucker. And I am not that lying bastard Helms."

"Richard Helms only lies in the interest of national security. And don't you use that gutter language in the oval office."

"Listen you motherfucker, give me the fucking President before I break your ass."

That enraged General Haig. He thought the pervert wanted to take his general's stars away. Haig slammed down the phone without even saying goodbye.

"Who was that, General?" The President was curious about the call.

"Just another one of those obscene phone calls, Mr. President. A sick person who thought he was that purveyor of smut, Hugh Hefner."

"Listen, whatever your name is, we've got enough trouble with the press without you pissing off one of the finest publishers in the land. Suppose it really was Hugh Hefner?"

"Hefner is a pervert."

"Call him back and apologize. That's an order."

So General Haig called Hugh Hefner and apologized. He also arranged for Miss February to be escorted to the POW Ball by Little Lamar

By May of l973 Hanoi began to work like a real town. It still looked like the South Bronx, but the flower market was open. And goods started appearing in the stalls lining Friendship of Nations Road--goods that haven't been seen in many a year. Why, you could actually buy an inner tube for a Schwinn in the Central Market. No child under twelve could remember the day when inner tubes were sold in the Central Market. The town was being repaired.

The one-man air raid shelters were filled in and flame trees planted in the fill. The red blossoms were just coming out and the air smelled sweet. Foreign ships started arriving in Haiphong Harbor. The ships brought long embargoed mail and packages and goods of all kinds. It was a happy time in Hanoi.

Mrs. Le Duc Tho was happy, more or less. Le Duc Tho managed to get hold of a prefabricated Albanian hen house. The hen house was erected on the site of the bombed flat villa. The erection took less than an hour. It was very comfortable as hen houses go. The main drawback was the lack of a kitchen. Mrs. Le Duc Tho had to cook the family meals outside, squatting next to an open char-coal fire. Still as Mrs. Le Duc Tho said, "It beats the old Imperial."

Mrs. Le Duc Tho was glad to get her mail. It had been a long time since she had received her copy of Elle. She had long subscribed to Elle, Le Monde, Le Figaro and L'Express. She was a great reader and liked to keep up with things. She thought Hanoi a little provincial and the Paris papers made her feel a part of things. She collected the recipe cards from Elle. She was glad to get some new ideas for supper.

Le Duc Tho was very happy. The war was over. He was living well within his salary. He had a small garden out back of the Albanian hen house. He enjoyed working in his garden. The hen house provided all the shelter he and Mrs. Le Duc Tho needed. He hated hotels. He managed to get his bicycle tires repaired and could cycle to work. He saved over an hour a day by cycling. He was very happy, very happy until the day the mail arrived. Le Duc Tho left work a little early that day. The garden needed a lot of weeding. Mrs. Le Duc Tho was reading a back copy of Le Monde. Tho picked up a copy of L'Express and turned to the section called Monde. He turned about as pale as an oriental individual can turn. He hid L'Express under one of the incubators.

He was very nervous. He said, "Honey, why don't ·we go out for dinner tonight? The restaurants are open in the park."

"That's sweet of you Tho, but I'd rather read the papers. Maybe after awhile. There is something in Le Monde about Henry Kissinger I'd like to read."

"Who cares about Henry Kissinger? I wouldn't read about him if I were you." Le Duc Tho was fishing for some diazepam. "It says here that Henry Kissinger was given the Nobel Peace Prize."

"It's often given to the wrong person. Besides it's just a dopey medal. I doubt if it's real gold."

"Le Monde thinks the prize is $1,000,000.00 in American money. Sounds like a lot of money. How much is that in piasters, Tho?"

"I don't know." He did so too. Le Duc Tho was as pale as an albino.

"If they gave the Nobel Peace Prize to anyone, it should have been you, honey."

"Aren't you getting hungry?"

"I don't believe it. I just don't believe it."

"There's fresh carp in the market. The restaurant in the park does wonderful carp."

"I don't believe it. I just don't believe it. Mother was night."

"Maybe your mother would like to go out to dinner with us."

"I don't believe it."

"I mean it. She'd be welcome. I'll pay. "

"Tho, did you turn down the Nobel Peace Prize and $1,000,000.00 in American money? Because if you did..."

"I don't deserve the Nobel Prize."

"Tho, it says right here in Le Monde that you turned down $1,000,000 .00. "

"Le Monde is a capitalist paper. Capitalists can't stand someone who turns down money."

"Do you realize what we could buy with $1,000,000.00? Why, that must be over a million piasters."

"We have everything we need."

"Everything we need and then some. You're a fool, Tho. Everything we need and then some. I'm always tripping over the goddamn brooder and that stupid incubator. I hit my head on the fucking roost. Tho, we 're living in a goddamn Albanian hen house. I don't even have a kitchen. And you say we don't need anything. I bet Doctor Kissinger doesn't live in a fucking Albanian hen house. Nancy showed me the pictures of her kitchen. It's bigger than our whole fucking chicken coop."

"It is a very comfortable hen house. "

Le Duc Tho had to sleep on his own side of the bed for the next three weeks. He never ever read a copy of Le Monde again.

"Mr. Nickleman please, Dick Westcott calling."

"Dick, what are you doing calling during the day? I thought you were trimming your expenses."

"I am, I am, Nickleman, but I've got one hot goddamn idea, and we'll have to move fast. You'll never believe it. "

"Try me."

"You remember those bracelets?"

"The POW bracelets? Shit yeah, they were my idea."

"Well, we got eighteen mailbags full of them this morning. It's unbelievable. The statistician says based on a Poisson distribution of mail arrivals we should get between thirty and forty tons of bracelets if nothing else is done. Of course it could be the top of an Erlang, but he doubts it." Dick Westcott had long hired statisticians to predict workloads and for various sampling techniques. In a really sweet deal, Dick Westcott used three or four statisticians and a demographer.

"Sounds like you'll have to beef up the mailroom."

"No, no, no, listen, I've been on the honker and most of the people are sending the bracelets back to the POW himself. Why, that toad Sloan got 586 pounds of them in Valdosta according to your friend BiBob."

"That Sloan has caused a lot of trouble. Just ask the Sweet Pea. Still in all, I think that he is the only POW worth a shit."

"Listen to what I'm trying to say, Nickleman. Everyone is mailing their bracelets somewhere. The fucking Post Offices are going crazy. There's talk of suing IT&T and Pitney-Bowes. At any rate it is just the dummies that don't know what else to do that are mailing the fucking bracelets back here. We'll have to head the POWs off. I got Gannett and The News to stop printing the addresses. I didn't bother with the fucking New

York Times. I gave Hearst and the wire services some shit about privacy, so we're OK there."

"Get to the point, Westcott."

"We're gonna have all fifteen fucking million of 'em mailed right back here, along with a dollar bill for each and every goddamn one."

"That's a lot of bracelets. "

"You bet your ass, 468 and one-quarter tons of them and fifteen million dollar bills. It's messy and singles are bulky, but we could skim more than half. We can bank them at the Little Commanders and get the money out of the country via Swiss Imports."

"Just why the fuck would anybody want to mail their bracelets back? Shit, they paid 9.95 plus 1.05 for postage and handling. You don't really expect people to mail them back along with a buck, do you?

"Fucking aye. For some reason everybody took into their head to mail the bracelets back when their guy came home. It is kind of a group consciousness thing, you know, like flying saucers. Remember we're not dealing with your normal person. These POW freaks are very easy to influence. Their minds are made of rice pudding. The statistician claims that, without prompting, fifty, maybe sixty percent of them will be mailed back. Shit, with prompting maybe ninety or even ninety-five percent. Well, Rubin Askew has already mailed his and his stickers. It will be the biggest yield in history. I mean we've got all the names in the computer. That and a few ads will bring back eight-to-one in dollar bills. Phenomenal, better than the Yangtze River flood. "

"What's the catch?"

"None; no catch. Now here is the beauty part, we'll commission a memorial monument made of the bracelets, you know, something like the Ben Franklin thing made out of pennies in Philly. A great Nixon head with an eternal flame out of the top. Nixon would like that. It would bug the Kennedys."

"Jesus Christ, a 468 ton asshole's head."

"Yeah, the fucking nose alone will weigh 60 tons."

"We just might get away with it, Dick."

"That's not all, maybe we could get one of the foundations, you know, Ford, Rockefeller, Mellon, Guggenheim, one of them, to foot the bill for the sculptor, or maybe a contest with an entry fee. The possibilities are unlimited."

"Let it roll then. Say, are you sure you've given up on the Sahara?"

"Yeah, fuck 'em, let 'em starve."

"Listen Nixon, you've gotta give me your private number. It is embarrassing dialing 202-456-1414 and going through all your flunkies just to talk with you. It was bad enough having to go through Haldeman."

"I am really very sorry about that, Mr. Hefner. But it is all these obscene telephone calls on my private lines. It's not like the COSMIC DELTA line. Say maybe I should get you a COSMIC DELTA phone."

"You should do just that. I can't stand that flunky that answers your phone. I really think he's a pervert. And I know a thing or two about perversion myself. Why, you should read some of my mail. And you'd never believe some of the pictures I get. A bunch of Amazon acrobats, some of 'em. Weird. Say, who is that bastard that answers your phone?"

"General Haig or something like that. He is a fine man and a wonderful general. He does keep talking about my considering the mood of the country. He's a great joker. "

"First let us straighten out this thing about Lamar Butte, then I'll help you settle this obscene phone call business."

"What about Little Lamar? He is a fine soldier." Mr. Nixon admired Little Lamar.

"That's the point. Little Lamar is just a soldier, a fucking corporal, a goddamn grunt. I can't have Miss February going to the POW Ball with a fucking corporal. Just think how that would look."

"It would be wrong, that's for sure. I'll talk to old what's his name about it."

"Talk, shit. Do something about it."

"Would you feel better if Miss November went to the POW Ball with a captain?"

"Yeah, get Miss February a captain. It is Miss February, Mr. Nixon, not Miss November. Miss November is black."

"We couldn't have that, could we?"

"I'll tell you what, Mr. Hefner, I'll make Little Lamar a captain. After all I'm the Commander-in-Chief. I can do anything I want. Would that do?" It would do. President Nixon promoted Little Lamar to captain. Little Lamar was made a captain in the Signal Corps. Later, much later, Little Lamar was put in charge of communications in Cambodia during what became known as the Mayaguez affair. The Mayaguez affair was the then President Jerry Ford's finest hour. Communications were hopelessly botched and the whole thing was a disaster. President Ford gave Little Lamar one of the highest medals a grateful nation can bestow. He also promoted Little Lamar to the rank of full bird colonel.

"Miss February would be pleased to go to the POW thing with Captain Lamar Butte. Now then, you said something about obscene phone calls."

"Yes, they are really bugging me. I don't know what the country is coming to."

"I know. Say, I've got a lot of friends in the obscene phone call business. I'll check it out." Check it out was one of Hugh Hefner's favorite expressions. Check it out he did.

And sure enough Hugh Hefner found the source of all the obscene phone calls. In the men's rooms of the many YMCAs around the country, Mr. Hefner found this message printed on the crapper walls: "If you want a blow job call 202-393-7101. If you can think of something better call 202-634-1507." 393-7101 was, as Mr. Hefner will tell you, the private number for the oval office. John Connally might remember 634-1507 as the private number of Mr. Nixon's crapper. Different YMCAs and quite a few Greyhound bus stations had different numbers, but the numbers were all numbers for the various private phones. All of the obscene calls were made in good faith. It was a mean thing for Ike Tapem to do. Just think of all the money the perverts wasted.

There is considerable disagreement amongst social historians as to which was the most vulgar event held at the White House during the Nixon presidency. Vulgarity is a matter of some subjectivity. Vulgarity is more a matter of statistics than a matter of moral philosophy. I am ill prepared to write on the subject of statistics or moral philosophy for that matter. I do know that all of the tabulations of vulgar events during the Nixon years included the night the POWs came to dinner. The POW thing (Nixon's designation, not mine) is mentioned in every monograph, in every doctoral thesis and in every popular book on the subject of presidential vulgarity. If that dinner was the most vulgar in an administration unmatched for vulgarity, then the POW thing must have been very vulgar indeed.

It was.

All the ex-POWs came, every last one. And almost all of them wore mess jackets and cummerbunds and little clip-on bow ties. The few enlisted men even wore mess jackets. It was the first time in living memory. It is true that G. David Schine had a mess jacket, but he wore it only in private. Private G. David Schine is a man of unimpeachable taste. Just ask Roy Cohn.

Mr. Nixon wore what he called a tux. It was in fact a dinner jacket. He wore an elaborate and elegant baby blue polyester dress shirt, which he frequently preened. When he preened, he looked like an elderly fag.

Invited to the POW thing were a number of actors or rather entertainers. At the thing was John Wayne. He is a fine American. It is said that he has appeared in a number of motion pictures. His nickname is Duke. What that has to do with Americanism, I really couldn't say.

A person by the name of Bob Hope was there. It is said that he is funny. That is to say humorous. He is a close friend of Mr. Nixon and has a similar nose.

A person by the name of Sammy Davis, Jr. was there. It is said that he is black. Many people deny this to be true.

Irving Berlin was there. This was a surprise to everyone. Most people thought him dead these many years. People said, "I thought he was dead."

Frank Sinatra (a crooner) might have been invited and could have been there. But nobody remembers seeing him. Several reliable witnesses assured me they would have noticed Mr. Sinatra had he been there.

There were a group of young women called Playmates. The Playmates were there on Mr. Nixon's explicit orders. The Playmates helped people off with their coats and passed peanuts and things like that. They were there in the interest of vulgarity. To that end, the Playmates wore old-fashioned dance hall girl costumes. Their brassieres pouted their breasts like so many passenger pigeons. The top edges of their nipple's areolae showed over the tops of the dance hall girl costumes. Some of the Playmates were quite modest and covered the slight peeks of their areolae with pancake make up.

All the ex-POWs to the man were in Washington for the POW thing. All the wives were there except Estelle Sloan. Sloan himself almost didn't come. Estelle was in Haiti getting a divorce. She almost gave in and came to the grand POW dinner. It would have been the high water mark of her life. "Dinner at the White House, just think of it, she would say. Estelle admired Richard Nixon then and she admires him now. Never say a critical word about Diehard Nixon around Estelle. If you do, Estelle will surely say, "I will not allow anyone to speak badly of the President. Please leave." Estelle Sloan would have done almost anything to go to the Nixons for dinner. Anything, that is, except fuck John H. Sloan. When she thought of having to do it, she started puking all over again. It was worse than before. It went on and on. Finally the father had to insert a suppository containing 25mg of prochlorperazine to stop the nausea. Estelle decided then and there never to see John ever again.

"Get a divorce, Estelle," said the father. And Estelle was doing just that on the day of the POW thing.

John H. Sloan almost didn't come, but the Air Force sent a Jetstar II to fetch him and Little Lamar. Had Little Lamar not lived in Valdosta, I rather doubt that the Air Force would have sent the Jetstar II for Sloan. Sloan had become a non-person at the Pentagon. They didn't know what they were going to do about him and were ignoring him. Had Sloan known what was going to happen to him at the White House, I can assure you that he would have stayed put at the Holiday Inn out on the new Statenville Road. But he didn't know. He wanted to visit the Army Personnel Assignment Office (APAO) and get an assignment. He wanted to get back to soldiering in the worst way. His leave had expired and no duty orders had arrived. Sloan called APAO every day. APAO always put him on hold and forgot about him. The hold button at the Pentagon does not play music.

Sloan was going crazy in Valdosta. Valdosta, a boring, hopeless place at best, is impossible for a guilty-feeling POW. John H. Sloan was the only guilty-feeling POW. Kleinschmidt's guilt vanished with the appearance of his first paycheck. At $175,000.00 a year reckons out to $14,583.33 a month. And if $14,583.33 a month won't take care of guilt, I don't know what will. Kleinschmidt passed the time seducing young women. Sloan passed the time grieving and wondering about Estelle worrying about Leavenworth and the doom that was sure to come, and drinking gin, lots of gin.

Father Francis X. McNaughton, S.J. was put in charge of quartering all of the ex-POWs, their wives, the entertainers, the Playmates, the crooners, the girlfriends and Miss February. Mr. Nixon took personal interest in the quartering and met with Father McNaughton every day. Father McNaughton booked first-class places for all. The entertainers and crooners got suites at the best hotels. Colonel John H. Sloan had a deluxe double room on the fifth floor of the Statler Hilton. Little Lamar had a single room on the seventh floor. Miss February was staying at the Mills-Hyatt House. Now the Mills-Hyatt House is a first-class hotel, but it is called, for some reason, a house. General King and Mrs. King were put up at Blair House, which really is a house. The taxpayers maintain Blair House for visiting dignitaries and ex-presidents. President Harry S. Truman stayed there when Bess was doing over the White

House. Very swanky is Blair House. Kleinschmidt and Karen Schuster were staying at the old Wardman-Park. Father McNaughton reserved them rooms on separate floors.

All of the POWs except Little Lamar were waiting for White House limousines to collect them. Little Lamar couldn't comprehend collection by a limousine. Such a thought never entered his mind. A lot of thoughts never entered his mind. He dressed carefully in his new mess jacket. The Army mess jacket was not designed with a slight humpback in mind. Little Lamar looked like a miniature Quasimodo. He remembered to put a clean handkerchief in his back pocket. His mother always said, "Little Lamar, always carry a clean handkerchief." He put on a brand new pair of boxer undershorts. One need not be a boxer to wear boxer undershorts. He didn't put them on to impress Miss February. That was another thought that didn't enter his mind. He put on the new undershorts to impress the undertaker. Mrs. Lamar Butte, Sr. used to say, "Lamar always wear clean underwear. What would the undertaker think?" Little Lamar always heeded his mother's advice.

Her advice was not always that good. For example, Little Lamar was not only the only 1188, but the only Army captain (homosexuals excepted) that had never fucked. Little Lamar had never even masturbated. He had had wet dreams from time to time, but he never woke up in time. Every time Little Lamar had an erection, his mother would say, "Don't do that Little Lamar. It will make you crazy." Still in all, Little Lamar liked the feel of an erection. He also worried about becoming crazy.

Little Lamar took the L-1 bus to the Mills -Hyatt House for his date with Miss February. The L-1 was the wrong bus. The L-1 bus is the bus for minor civil servants traveling to Chevy Chase. Chevy Chase, by the way, has nothing to do with chasing the brand of automobile sold by Big Bob. Most other civil servants were riding the bus because their wives wanted the car that day. The Chevy Chase bound civil servants looked at Little Lamar, shook their heads and went back to reading The

Washington Star. There was a special section about the grand POW thing.

The special section had a complete list of the people invited.

More was promised for the next day. One of the civil servants, a man from the State Department's Protocol Division, thought Little Lamar must be a footman from one of the South American embassies.

Little Lamar pushed the button on his brand new digital watch and went pale. He should be at the Mills-Hyatt House by now. He asked the bus driver how long before we get to the Mills-Hyatt House? The bus driver answered, "You're on the wrong bus, buddy."

"But I've got a date with Miss February. I'm taking her to the POW thing." Sometimes Little Lamar knows the right thing to say. He is very smart for an 1188.

"You a POW, buddy? You don't look like one." Then he saw what a sorry looking human being Little Lamar was and said, "It must have been tough. Those fucking Commies, I'd like to get just one of them on the old L-1. I'd fix his ass."

Little Lamar looked ever so unhappy. The bus driver stopped the bus and called the District of Columbia Police.

With sirens screaming, Little Lamar got to the Mills-Hyatt House only five minutes late. Up the elevator and into Miss February's suite went Little Lamar. There, waiting was Miss February. She was prettier than her picture. Her picture for some reason is called a centerfold. Her dress was only slightly less revealing. Hot only did her areolae show, both goddamn nipples were there to see. Little Lamar had never seen such a sight. Never had he seen such a beautiful girl, live. He didn't know what to say and went cross-eyed.

Little Lamar's penis started getting bigger and bigger and still bigger. It was the biggest erection Little Lamar ever had had.

For a little man, Little Lamar has a very big penis indeed. It is not just a matter of scale. When his penis stands erect it is quite a sight to see.

Miss February saw it and said, "Wow."

Little Lamar didn't know what to say or do. He wished for some schoolbooks to hold in front of him. He couldn't think of a single thing to do or say. All he could do was look cross-eyed and wish that his erection would go away. There are at least three things that Little Lamar could do. He tried none of them.

He just looked cross-eyed and smiled at Miss February.

Miss February couldn't think of anything to say. She never could. This is not because she had never seen an erection. She had seen and taken care of hundreds upon hundreds of them. She had spent a good deal of time making thousands of penises erect. Miss February had about as much interest in sex as Little Lamar had knowledge of that subject. That is not to say she had never fucked. She had fucked perhaps 5000 times. But it was just something she did, like getting up in the morning. The reason Miss February fucked so much and so often was simple. She could never think of anything to say, so she fucked. She could pass for a very good- looking 1188. After 5000 fucks, she learned a few words and said, "You just save that until later."

"Save what?" answered Little Lamar.

"This." And Miss February put her hand right on Little Lamar's great penis.

"You 1 re going to make me crazy." Little Lamar was dead serious. He was scared of going crazy and he thought this was the way. He had never felt this way or this good before.

"All you men say that. Say, you're cute." Miss February stroked Little Lamar's penis.

Little Lamar now knew he was going crazy. He ejaculated like Mount Etna. He ejaculated all over his boxer shorts and his brand new trousers. Little Lamar convulsed with the new pleasure. Even Miss February had never seen an orgasm like this.

She worried that Little Lamar might be having an epileptic fit. Little Lamar was sure that he was in the very act of going crazy. He thought his brains were coming out through his penis. He shook for a full minute, then looked at Miss February and sobbed. "That's all right, baby," Miss February has a kind heart.

She wiped him off best she could. Little Lamar almost died of shame when Miss February unbuckled his belt and lowered his trousers. It took 10 of the Mills-Hyatt House towels to wipe him clean. Never had Miss February seen so much seminal fluid at one time. Little Lamar started getting hard again . "Wait until we get back, baby. It will be better next time."

"Better?" answered Little Lamar. He couldn't understand better. The hour was getting late. There was nothing else for them to do but leave for the White House, semen stained trousers and all.

The Kings were put up at Blair House by mistake. President Nixon told Father McNaughton, S.J., Put the King up in Blair House." Father McNaughton was not one to question the President's orders. Father McNaughton wasn't sure whether the President meant Frank Sinatra (the crooner) or General King. Both men were held in high regard around the White House. The President meant John Wayne, Duke John Wayne. The President in his usual fashion promoted John Wayne to king. But Father McNaughton put General and Mrs. Rex King in Blair House. And that is where they were.

General King was dressed and waiting for the White House limousine. He looked very smart in his handsome mess jacket with the gold stars on the shoulder boards. Regina King was dressed in her new evening dress. She looked like a DAR lady.

Regina was down in the kitchen of Blair House sneaking a small gin. She looked like a D.A.R. lady sneaking a small gin. Mrs. King was making the best of her bad lot and drinking gin when she could. Rex, as it turned out, did not grow more tender in prison. He was, if any- thing, more of a Christian. He called the peek-nique a harlot suit. "Get it out of my sight," said General King. So far the Kings had only had a few hard missionary Fucks. Mrs. King was grateful for the Vagilube. Rex remained ignorant of the Staylong ointment.

The ex-POWs didn't go directly to the White House. First they assembled at the new State Department Office Building. From there they shuttled the short distance to the White House in waves of limousines. It was a small inconvenience, but it insured a steady stream of POWs and vastly aided Father McNaughton's task of scheduling. All in all there were well over a thousand ex-POWs and their wives and girlfriends . This doesn't include the entertainers and crooners . It was   a terrible strain on the large fleet of White House limousines. The firs wave of ex-prisoners and their wives were the men promoted to admiral and general during their confinement . Lesser men would wait in the lobby of the new State Department Office Building. The entertainers and crooners were accorded equal privileges with the flag officers.

The arrivals were coordinated by Father McNaughton. Father McNaughton and his small staff of radio operators assured a steady flow of admrals and generals and entertainers. As the guests drove up the circular driveway, one of the many bands played the Washington Post March. It was a small joke by a daring bandmaster.

The first wave assembled in the main lobby of the White House. The trumpeters gave a fanfare on grotesque trumpets. The head White House usher shouted, "Ladies and gentlemen, the President of the United States of America."

A specialized band came forth with Ruffles and Flourishes and then Hail to the Chief. Dum, dum, dump, te, dump, dumpty, dumpty, dumpty dump.

At the top of the great staircase appeared not the President and his lady, but two flag bearers flanked by two marines carrying Springfield rifles. Mr. Nixon didn't know that the rifles were called Springfield rifles, nor did he know that Springfield was a town in Massachusetts. Good thing, too. Mr. Nixon hated Massachusetts and there is no telling what he would have done with this knowledge.

The band played another bar of Hail to the Chief as the colors started down the stairs. "When Hail to the Chief came around again, the President and his lady appeared. The President flashed a "V" sign with both hands. The crowd of admirals and generals and entertainers and crooners clapped wildly. The President's palms faced in. The President did not know that when the "V' sign for victory is given, the palms should face out. The two gestures have quite different meanings. It was the same mistake that got Harvey Smith in so much trouble with the judges at the Badminton trials. He was disqualified for making obscene gestures at the judges after he won the trials. Harvey Smith claimed he didn't know there was a difference; the President really didn't know. Mr. Nixon thought himself the greatest President ever. Harvey Smith is the greatest steeplechase rider ever.

A reception line was formed and the admirals and generals were rushed through while the limousines went back for the next wave.

Father McNaughton held up the shuttle of limousines until the President and Mrs. Nixon could tromp back up the stairs to start the whole cycle over again for the Navy captains and Air Force colonels. The trumpeters wet their lips and readied themselves.

The third wave, the majors and below waited in the vestibule of the new State Department Office Building. The crowd had thinned. There weren't all that many low ranking ex-prisoners after all those prison promotions. Some of the popular men, the ones that photographed well and had appeared on television talk shows received more promotions since coming home.

Kleinschmidt and Miss Schuster were chatting idly. It was the first time Kleinschmidt had seen Miss Schuster socially since San Francisco. He ran out of things to say to her. Karen had thought of something new and was trying to explain it to Justin.

Justin was paying little attention and was looking around. He spotted Little Lamar. Actually he spotted Miss February first. Then he spotted Little Lamar. He shouted across the vestibule, "Hi there, baby tuckoo."

"He a nicen little boy," answered Little Lamar. Little Lamar wasn't sure he was all that nice. His mother's words rang in his ears. Still he felt pretty wonderful.

It was time to go. Kleinschmidt hollered, "Ride with us, baby tuckoo." The luck of the draw gave them Ziegler's limousine. Kleinschmidt rolled the windows down to let some fresh air in. His hand brushed across Miss February 's nipples. Miss February didn't notice. Karen Schuster smiled at Miss February, and Miss February did notice the smile and squeezed Little Lamar 's hand. Miss February felt pretty wonderful. Justin Kleinschmidt was a little cross-eyed.

They arrived at the White House. A White House usher with the rank of major in the United States Marine Corps quietly asked Kleinschmidt for his name. Kleinschmidt uncrossed his eyes and said, "Littlesmith."

"General Wellborne, may I present Captain and Mrs. Littlesmith." Karen Schuster wasn't Mrs. Littlesmith or even Mrs. Kleinschmidt for that matter, but never mind. General Wellborne wears the gold aiguillettes of a Presidential aide. He still calls it a fourragere.

Kleinschmidt and Miss Schuster proceeded down the receiving line. Each dignitary becoming grander and more important than the last. They were always introduced as Captain and Mrs. Littlesmith. The grander the eminence; the triter his comment. Miss Schuster, with her long experience on receiving lines on Long Island (Long Island is a very long island) at bar mitzvahs, weddings and the like, knew no one paid the slightest attention to what was said. She said, "Up yours," to a tall, thick-at-the-waist, toupeed, aging entertainer with a noble title.

She told George Nickleman that he looked like her grandmother. George Nickleman's feelings were deeply hurt.

Dr. Kissinger was greeted with, "Physician, heal thyself."

Mrs. Littlesmith only thought she was clever. In the interest of good taste, her comments to one Sammy Davis, Jr. will not be recorded on these pages.

One man, an Air Force four star general, was introduced as: "The man who ended the war. " It seems the general was the Air Force general in charge of AFOPs and as such was in charge of the Christmas bombing. Kleinschmidt asked, "Do you mean to say that they gave the Nobel Peace Prize to the wrong person? "

No one got it, not even the clever Miss Schuster.

Miss Schuster was struck dumb when she was introduced to the President of the United States of America. Her wit left. Her left hand automatically started scratching her right collarbone. All things sexual embarrass President Nixon. If anything at all, he is an ass man, not a tit man. A careful reading of the Presidential papers will support this hypothesis. While there is little doubt that the President is an ass man, there is no truth whatsoever to the widely held belief that this was the reason for picking that fellow Agnew as his Vice President. Still, it must be admitted that no other plausible reason has been advanced.

Still in all, Miss Schuster's breasts were quite the best pair of knockers, as Mr. Nixon liked to call them, that this President had ever seen. The Playmates' knockers were pushed up under their chins. The swollen blue veins, to this ass man, were repugnant. He was not turned on, as they say in the titillation business. Miss Schuster's knockers aren't bad thought the President. Mr. Nixon avoided looking cross-eyed.

The President Nixon is a tightly controlled man. He rarely bothers to look someone in the eye. Maybe he finds it painful. As Colonel Sloan came down the line he looked Sloan in the eye by mistake. The President winced, then stiffened. He looked like a man trying ever so hard to hold back a fart during a minute of silent prayer. The President assumed that Sloan, that turncoat, that toad, would not be invited. Nickleman would really catch it in the morning. Still the President retained control and presumably the fart and hissed, "Give him the shaft. " We'll find out what the shaft is later.

There were 101 tables of twelve and one table, a raised dais, seating forty. The dinner was to honor the former POWs. One could suppose that the dais would have as many honorees as could comfortably fit. If you supposed that, you are wrong. The places were occupied by the host and Mrs. Nixon, a crooner, the elder entertainers and their wives and/or girlfriends. The only POW at that table was Little Lamar. He was seated next to Miss February. He was very happy and took no notice of anyone save Miss February. I should point out that Mr. Nixon personally approved the seating plan. I heard that some of the entertainers were grumpy at having to sit next to their wives (or girlfriends) all evening.

Round the 101 tables were two dozen small bars. Scattered in even greater numbers were Grumman canoes full of ice and champagne. Kleinschmidt was partial to the Ouachita canoes from Philadelphia, Arkansas. But, there is no whitewater at the White House, so what difference does it make? Also, Ouachita is not a defense contractor.

Each table had a Filipino waiter, all Navy mess stewards, it was said. The folks on the dais had a waiter, also Navy mess stewards, for each two eminences. I couldn't count the dozens and dozens of bus boys.

The Filipinos shuttled back and forth to the Grumman canoes for the California champagne. New York State champagne, say Taylors, Great Western or Cook, is much the better wine. This idea was vetoed by President Nixon who said, "New Yorkers are a bunch of Jews and liberals, you know, intellectuals. Fuck 'em."

The President himself drank Dom Perignon. He read about that wine in a James Bond book.

Kleinschmidt, Miss Schuster, Colonel Sloan, an empty chair, the CIA pilot and his wife and six other people were seated together. I am embarrassed to say I spilled gin on my notes containing those six other people's names. But as I recall, the names have no bearing on this story.

Sloan beckoned one of the Filipinos. "Mr. Manolo, what is your first name? "

"That is my first name, sir."

Sloan was puzzled, but came around.

"What is your last name then?"

"Rivera y El Rey, sir. "

"Well, Mr. Rivera, er, ah, ah, King, I really don't like this bubbly stuff. Could you bring me a gin?"

"Yes sir, what sort of gin, sir? "

"A Gin Thomas. That is gin, soda and lemon--no sugar." The drink Gin Thomas is named after Clive Thomas of Aiken, South Carolina.

Kleinschmidt slipped Mr. Rivera y El Rey $20 in American money and said, "Keep the Major's, er, the Colonel's glass full. He looks like he needs it." How true. John H. Sloan looked worried. He was harried. And not without reason.

Manolo had never been tipped in his four years at the White House. Ho one was ever tipped at the White House, except for the hatcheck person. The hatcheck person was a Navy woman. She saved the quarter toward her summer holiday. She planned a five-day cruise to Nassau. She had never been to sea and was looking forward to what she called the experience. Manolo planned to and indeed bought more shoeshine kits with his twenty dollars.

General and Mrs. King sat at a table with five other generals and their wives. Some of the generals and their wives were drinking California champagne. Some were drinking gin. The insecure ones were drinking Scotch. General King was drinking Tab. Mrs. King was wishing for some gin, When Manolo Rivera y El Rey whisked by on his way for another Gin Thomas, Mrs. King caught his eye. "Oh hello, Missy. How are you? "

"Just fine, if only you could bring me a glass of tea. You know like you fixed for me on the Jetstar." Mrs. King winked.

"Tea?" answered General King. "Jetstar? What Jetstar? "

Mrs. King tried time after time to tell Rex about the Jetstar trip and the oval office visit. General King would not hear it. Or General King so loved President Nixon that he gave his only begotten wife little attention. The Jetstar trip and the oval office meeting didn't exist for him.

"Tea?" said Manolo Rivera y El Rey.

"You know, like Missy likes." Mrs. King was winking like a Bell's palsy victim.

"Oh yes, Missy. Manolo knows."

Manolo Rivera y El Rey is a fine man. From then on every time he passed Mrs. King's table he dropped off a large gin and Tab. You will be happy to hear that seven months later Manolo retired on a large pension and returned to the Philippines. He said upon arrival, "I have returned." Never again did he have to call an American lady "Missy." Never again did he have to shine anyone's shoes. Never again did he have to bring anyone a gin or a Sanka. He married a very pretty girl, bought a fine house and lives very happily. His wife brings him a San Miguel beer whenever he asks.

You will not be happy to hear about the Kings. It is my sad duty to say, as of this writing, Mrs. King still must sneak her gin and use Vagilube whenever Rex can get it up. Luckily, Rex is often off on a speaker's program called Speak Out for Christ. Rex 's only complaint is the buttons on the pink prin-cess touchtone telephone.

The menu was simple as White House dinners. There was no appetizer, game, salad, fruit or cheese course. Mr. Nixon would not allow soup to be served at the White House. The first course, according to the printed menu, was Seafood Neptune. It was perversity. It was an amalgam of crab, shrimp and scallops bound together with case-hardened Campbell's cream of mushroom soup. The Seafood Neptune was heated in the White House kitchen; it was put together by a caterer in New York.

The vegetable course was called Hearts of Palm. It was in fact swamp cabbage from the little town of Mayo in Lafayette County, Florida. Swamp cabbage keeps rather well without refrigeration, but one of the large specialty food firms quick-froze it. Some teamsters alternatively thawed and refroze the swamp cabbage on its way north. The swamp cabbage had no tooth by the time it was served on the south lawn.

The third course was perhaps the most honestly named. It was Roast Beef au jus according to the printed card. It was roast beef, but it had sat on the warming table long enough for the au jus to adieu. The resourceful White House chef ordered the use of canned gravy. The patisserie objected. "Fuck 'em," said the chef.

There were many toasts. Hymns were sung. A croup of parachutists gave the President an elaborate plaque engraved with the words: OUR LEADER, OUR COMRADE, and RICHARD THE LION HEARTED.

Yes, the parachutists gave Richard the Lion Hearted a plaque, but Richard the Lion Hearted was going to give Sloan the shaft. Sloan heard Nixon's order. Richard Nixon doesn't whisper efficiently. Sloan drank his Gin Thomases and worried about what form the shaft would take. The shaft was an Administrative Corrections Discharge DOD Form 237Y34321.831 Rev 2.8. It was mailed without comment to the Holiday Inn out on the New Statenville Road. An Administrative Corrections Discharge doesn't sound that bad. It doesn't sound bad at all until you read DOD Directive 8183910 .987-5 Rev. 89.45. Buried in Part 8, Chapter 42, subsection 57, paragraph 7 you will find that an Administrative Corrections Discharge annuls all records of a man's service. It is as if Sloan had never been in the Army. The Army now supposed Sloan never to have joined. If he never joined, he could not have been promoted to colonel. If he was not a colonel, he could not receive a colonel's pay and allotments. If he had never been in the Army, he could not retire. If he could not retire, he could not receive his retirement pay.

And that, dear reader is the shaft.

Little Lamar and Miss February were holding hands and looking longingly into each other's eyes. Neither ate or drank a thing at the POW thing. I am pleased to report that on that very night Little Lamar and Miss February engaged in sexual congress at the Hills-Hyatt House. Miss February had her first orgasm ever. She looked at Little Lamar and said, "Oh, Little Lamar, I love you."

Little Lamar thought if this were crazy, it ain't bad, and said, "Will you marry me? "

"Oh, yes, Little Lamar." Miss February held Little Lamar's penis in her right hand. His penis was on the rise. "Little Lamar, you're not so little. Where have you been all my life? "

"Around," said Little Lamar.

Three days a Justice of the Supreme Court married later Miss February and Little Lamar. The Justice was a strict constructionist. He constructed a fine marriage. President Richard M. Nixon was the best man. Hugh Hefner gave the bride away.

When last I talked to Colonel Lamar Butte, Jr. and his beautiful wife February, they seemed very happy. February said, "I've never been so happy. "

And that is the end of the story.

"You can't end the story there."

Why not? Say, who are you?

"I am the editor. You can't just say that is the end of the story and quit."

Sorry, you surprised me. But it is my story and I should be able to quit anywhere I want. Besides the story is over. There is no more to say.

"You didn't finish the story. What happened to General Haig for example?"

He became the top general of the Western World. Head of NATO, I think. He is a very successful general. And that is the end of the story.

"You can't end the story there."

It is a sad ending, I know, but you asked for it. I like happy endings. What do you want for a lousy 3,000 bucks?

"We'll get it back if you end the story there. What happened to young Wellborne?"

He married a lovely girl, a Radcliffe graduate, an expert on the nomads of the Central and Western Sahara. She calls Wellborne Swifty.

"That isn't very nice of her."

He's not very nice. And that is the end of the story.

"Wait a minute. What about Nixon?"

Save me, please save me. Look, you can try to get your money back if I have to say another word about Nixon. Besides everybody knows that he lives in oriental splendor at taxpayers expense out in California. If you will leave me alone, I will say that he drives up to Los Angeles for Irish coffee sometimes. Ask me something else.

"What about Le Roy Kaiser?"

I'm really glad you asked about him. I am pleased to say that he won the lottery and lives on Park Avenue in great luxury. I didn't know how to work that in. That should end the story on a happy note. I like happy endings.

"Happy note or no happy note, you can't end the story there."

You're a tough editor, if ever I've seen one. What else do you want from me?

"Whatever happened to Pohn Van Ngo, Sr.?"

Well, as you might remember, he was made a Hero of the Peoples Republic of Vietnam.

"Of course; what kind of editor do you think I am?"

No offense. Hero of the Peoples Republic of Vietnam is more than a title. It entitles the hero to a four-room house with a cook shed out back. Pohn Van Ngo's house is right next door to Le Due Tho's hen house. They often play checkers together. Pohn's daughter-in-law married Nguyen Thanh Linh and they all live in Pohn Van Ngo's new house. Mrs. Le Duc Tho sometimes baby-sits for the Linh. Everyone is very happy. Mrs. Nguyen Thanh Linh is pregnant. And that is a happy ending; if ever I've told one. And that is the end of the story.

"Would you please stop saying, 'and that is the end of the story.' I'll tell you when to quit."

You are tough. What else do you want to know?

 "What do you have against Valdosta?"

Who ' s Valdosta?

"Valdosta, Georgia, you idiot!"

What about Valdosta, Georgia?

"You said some very unkind things about Valdosta."

I did?

"Yes, you called Valdosta a mean and miserable place."

I don't know how I could know that. Why, I've never even been to Valdosta. I'm sure that it is a lovely town. I'll catch a bus down there and check it out if you will advance me a hundred bucks or so for the ticket and a small amount of gin.

"What about the Le Due Thos?"

Let me see. Well, the incubator came in very handy in the wintertime. It keeps the hen house very cozy. Mrs. Le Duc Tho let her subscription to Le Monde and Le Figaro lapse. She still gets L'Express and Elle. She has a splendid collection of recipe cards. She checks L'Express each week to make sure Le Duc Tho doesn't turn down any more Nobel Prizes. She told Tho, "Tho, I'll have your ass if you turn down another Nobel Prize." Le Duc Tho lives in fear of the traditional early morning telephone call from Stockholm. That is about all I know. Le Duc Tho still rides his bike to work.

"OK, that's enough."

You want me to end the story there? Seems like an odd place, but it's A-OK with me.

"Stop being silly. Tell us about George Nickleman and Dick Westcott."

They got into the laetrile business and are making a fortune. It is a good subject for another book. If you will give me some money for typewriter paper and ribbons and food, rent and gin, I'll get started on it right away.

"Give me an outline. "

I'll get started on it this afternoon. And that is the end of the story.

"Stop saying that. What about Kissinger?"

What about him?

"What happened to him?"

It's all a matter of public record. He won't give me an interview, even though I am working on his biography. Briefly, he stayed on as Ford's man, and then went on to better things.

"That's too brief. "

He is very successful. He is paid millions of dollars to justify himself on television shows for NBC (a television network). He gets huge advances on his books. More than you give me, I might add. He's with some school. The name eludes me.

Goldman Sachs hired him, I think. I don't know where he finds the time. He is very successful, as I say. Any other details would be in poor taste.

 "Everything about your book is in poor taste. So why not finish it in poor taste? "

The things I have to put up with.

"What's that?"

Nothing. I was just thinking out loud. Will you leave me alone if I finish the story grossly?

"Yes."

Well, it seems Henry Kissinger pees about 1500cc of urine most days. His feces weigh, on the average 465 grams (dry weight). His blood lipids are a little high--cholesterol 360mg, phospholipids 36mg, triglycerides 2.0mg (all figures expressed per 100ml of blood after a twelve hour fast). His urobilinogen is less than1.0 Ehrlich u. which, as you know, is not all that bad. His BUN is 25mg/100ml, which is not bad. H is urea is BUN x 2.14, also acceptable. I could go on and on. Dr. Kissinger is slightly overweight for the maintenance of good health. He has an erection on the average of three times a week. He takes a bath when needed.

"Enough. Enough. "

OK. That is the end of the story. Kissinger is human.

The End.